ELISA ANN PRATT

Silver Linings: TRUTH

TRUTH

First published by Elisa Ann Pratt 2024

First edition

ISBN (paperback): 979-8-9894571-6-8
ISBN (hardcover): 979-8-9894571-7-5

This book was professionally typeset on Reedsy.
Find out more at reedsy.com

To my husband, children, family and friends
To my Mom who always believed in my talent as a writer
To my inner child who truly needed this story to come out
To my loyal readers and everyone who has supported me in this process
#ShareTeam - You all know who you are!
Most of all for anyone else out there who feels alone and scared. May you
be inspired by this story to find the light to a path where everything you
truly deserve comes to fruition.

With Love and Light,
Always
Elisa Ann Pratt

Contents

Foreword

For my fellow music lovers out there, the following songs have all been a great inspiration to this story. I truly hope you enjoy the following playlist as much as I do.

Book 1 - Silver Linings: DRAWN
  Live to Tell - Madonna
  Vision of Love - Mariah Carey
  Hungry Eyes - Eric Carmen
  Real Love - Mary J. Blige
  I wanna know what love is - Foreigner
  Iris - Goo Goo Dolls
  Lucky Star - Madonna
  Sweetest Taboo - Sade
  God blessed the broken road - Rascal Flatts

Book 2 - Silver Linings: SECRETS
  I'll be there for you - Bon Jovi
  Crazy for you - Madonna
  Nice and Slow - Usher
  Piano in the Dark - Brenda Russell
  Who Knew - Pink

Confessions - Usher
Alone - Heart
Angel - Aerosmith

Book 3 - Silver Linings: TRUTH
Live to Tell - Madonna
Since you been gone - Kelly Clarkson
What hurts the most - Rascal Flatts
Against all Odds - Phil Collins
She's like the wind - Patrick Swayze
Need you now - Lady Antebellum
You were meant for me - Jewel
No Ordinary Love - Sade
That's the way love goes - Janet Jackson
No more Drama - Mary J. Blige
What a feeling - Irene Cara
Heart of the Matter - Don Henley

Preface

This story contains sensitive material that may be disturbing to some readers for containing the following subjects: **abusive relationship, addiction, alcoholism, anxiety, sexual assault** and **sexually explicit content.** Reader discretion is advised.

Acknowledgments

Another Shout out to #ShareTeam - without your unwavering support, this trilogy
would not have found it's way into the hands of so many of my readers!
I love you all from the bottom of my heart and know that there was no way I could have made it through this journey without you all.

My amazing ARC Team! I have full faith that with your help, we can drive
Silver Linings: Truth forward in her success in the launch process.
I appreciate every single one of you for taking the time to read and review this story. Thank you all so much!
I truly hope you all enjoy it and look forward to hearing all of your thoughts.

Chapter 1

⁂

The party was a big hit! Jamie and Dillon pitched in on a new karaoke machine for my birthday. Everyone had a blast, taking turns to get up and sing their favorite songs. When the party was over, everyone went home wearing big smiles.

Jamie handed me the last of my gifts to put away, before she and Dillon went to bed for the night. I hung the satin, turquoise, cocktail gown I had received from Breana and Ryan in the closet and set the leather bound journal and pen set from Brooke and Jason on my nightstand. I had never used an I Pod before. Surely, I would need some help in loading my favorite songs onto the device, but I was extremely thankful to Alex and Mandy for the gift. I had always joked that music ran through my veins. A vessel, connecting me to my fondest of memories, music always had a special way of reminding me that I was not alone in this world, no matter how I was feeling.

My night was far from over. I still had Jasper waiting upstairs for me.

I had no idea he was going to surprise me and show up at my party. Jamie told everyone he was coming while I wasn't around and they all conspired to keep it a secret, leaving me clueless.

Before making the trip to be here, Jasper had a long day, working at his new lake house property. I didn't want to keep him waiting long, but I needed to take a moment of gratitude, as I glanced around at my birthday blessings. They were all such sweet and thoughtful gifts. Somehow, I managed to find my way inside their hearts. My new friends were all beginning to know me for who I truly was as a person. I was incredibly grateful for this new phase of my life. A time for new beginnings. I heard my phone chime and picked it up to find a text message from Jasper.

Jasper

Meet me upstairs in the loft when you get here.

Me

I'm coming. See you in a few!

Jasper

OK. Hurry.

Chapter 2

I gathered some clothes for the next day and loaded them into my overnight bag, along with my toothbrush and some other essentials. It was already after midnight, so I knew I would more than likely stay the night over at Jasper's place. I zipped up my bag and made a stop by the kitchen to pack up a few slices of my birthday cake to take with me and headed out the door.

I nearly forgot that Jasper gave me a new pin code for his apartment. It was no wonder why the elevator wouldn't budge when I put the old one in. I laughed to myself as entered the correct pin code. The elevator was magically brought to life and began it's climb to Jasper's penthouse.

When I reached the top floor, the elevator door opened and I walked inside. I could hear music streaming down from the loft upstairs. It was a classical piano piece I had never heard before, but alluring, nonetheless in its seductive notes. Recalling Jasper's request to meet him upstairs in the loft, I set the container of cake down on top of the kitchen island and made my way up the spiral staircase.

When I reached the top, I was greeted by the soft whimpers of one very large Lucas, who was tucked inside his crate for the night. I gave him a quick pat on the head through the wires of the crate and sat my overnight bag down on the coffee table. I took a seat on the white leather sofa and let out a yawn. By now, the alcohol from the wine was beginning to wear off and I was feeling a bit tired. If I weren't both nervous and excited to see Jasper, I probably would have crashed out on my bed and called it a night.

"I'm in here, come inside." I heard Jasper call out to me through the bathroom door that was left ajar.

"Okay, I'm coming." I called back. I rose to my feet to adhere to his request.

When I opened the bathroom door, the volume of the music increased inside my ears, setting the tone for the scene before me. All of my senses had awakened as I took in the scent of fresh roses that filled the air. Jasper was standing in the doorway that connected his bedroom to the bathroom in his favorite gray sweatpants. They were hung low, bringing my attention to the v in his perfectly sculpted hips. He had already removed his shirt and I nearly caught myself drooling at the sight of his strong arms and chiseled chest. I inhaled deeply to steady myself from losing my composure.

"Angel…." He said with that super sexy smirk of his. The soft dim light flickered in his eyes, revealing the deepest shade of sapphire blue I had ever seen. The jolt of electricity hit me like a freight train. Suddenly, my cheeks felt warm and I could feel my heart rate begin to climb in anticipation of his touch. I was at a loss for words, as always when his hunger for me radiated through the energy that surrounded him. He took a step towards me and my eyes caught sight of the Jacuzzi bath filled with rose petals, bubbling as the steam rose above the water.

"It's been a long day. I know *I* could use a soak in the hot tub... Would you care to join me?" He asked, his voice trailing off into a lusty whisper, as he walked over to where I was standing. Without waiting for my response, he took my hand in his and twirled me around. "You look stunning, Angel..." he breathed, "but this dress really needs to come off." He pushed my hair to the sides of my face to access the zipper that formed at the base of my neck. My words were so far from my voice, I couldn't help but let him begin to undress me. He pulled my dress down past my shoulders and waist, letting it fall to the floor. I was left standing there in nothing but my bra, panties and shoes.

"I've had you on my mind all week." He whispered against my neck before placing a soft kiss on my shoulder from behind. I felt a ripple of goosebumps rise to the surface of my skin as the butterflies in my core swarmed in delight. He made quick work of the snaps of my bra, as it fell, carelessly to the floor. With a soft trace against my ribs, he slid his fingers down to the sides of my panties and before I knew it, they too, were on the floor. I finally found my nerve to help out by slipping out of my shoes. I could feel Jasper watching me from behind as he removed his sweatpants and climbed inside the tub.

Sweeping my dress and panties up off the floor in as much grace as my body would allow in its full nude form, I carefully placed them onto the bathroom counter. I turned my focus to Jasper's sweatpants that were also lying on the ground.

"Leave it, Angel. Get in here, while the water is still warm." He chuckled. I heard the water swish around him. Empowered by his invitation, I quickly adhered to his command without second guessing myself. I felt so vulnerable, prancing around naked in his bathroom that the idea of getting inside the tub with him, soon became a welcoming deterrent.

I swung my leg over the rim to feel the temperature before completely immersing my body into the water. The tub was large enough to sit four adults comfortably. I flinched ever so slightly in adjustment to the water as it covered my belly and found a seat on the other side of the tub, adjacent to where Jasper was sitting. With our bodies concealed beneath bubbles and rose petals, I didn't feel so naked anymore. Jasper stared at me intently before splashing his way over to my side of the tub. The desire between us was thick enough to cut with a knife… I had to say something to break the intensity I was feeling.

"This is really nice." I said with my eyes fixed on the rose petals as they swirled through the jetted bubbles. "Do you always bathe in flowers?" I asked with a giggle.

"No." He laughed. "I was hoping you would like it," He said as he bridged the gap between us and slid himself behind me.

"Oh, I definitely do." I said, letting myself escape into the feeling of his wet skin against mine. The heat of the water had tarnished the red of the roses into a deep burgundy brown. Watching the petals tumble around gave me something to focus on, rather than my nerves that would otherwise be going haywire. *Am I really sitting in here, naked? With Jasper?*

"I'm glad you like it, Angel." Jasper said as he slid his hands over my arms and began kissing the back of my neck, forcing me to turn my head in response. I wanted his lips on mine so badly, I couldn't help myself from making the first move. He welcomed my advance by slipping his tongue inside my mouth, while simultaneously guiding me over to the other side where he could get better leverage. The water splashed over the rim and a few of the petals seeped out over the tub as our bodies collided with one another. I couldn't help my giggles from escaping me.

"Shh..." Jasper said with a chuckle of his own as he deepened our passionate kiss. He placed one of his hands on the back of the tub behind me and drew his other hand beneath the water to slide up my thigh. Smoothing his way over my hips, he crossed over to my rear to hold me in place.

His trailed his sweet, soft lips down my neck, while positioning me in a way that would expose my breast just above the surface of the water through the petals. He continued the trail of his mouth down to my left nipple as he teasingly gave it a gentle pinch between his fingers, making them stiffen to a hard peak. Fully immersing his mouth around my breast, he suckled as if I were to bleed honey.

Utilizing his free hand, he found his way to my sweet spot where he began massaging in circular motions. I could feel his erection growing firm at my knee when I released a pleasureful moan into his ear. I quickly returned his gesture by gripping his shaft in the palm of my hand as I gave it a gentle squeeze with my fingers. *Hello sailor!* I proceeded to work my hand in motion under the water and slid my thumb up over the tip of his penis while Jasper slid his fingers in and out of me. He brought his lips back up to mine and kissed me with enough passion to set my entire world on fire. My senses were going haywire. It wasn't very long before the magic unfolded between us as we both began our climb to our release. Jasper groaned in hesitance.

"Wait... Not here." Jasper breathed into my ear. I scooted back in the seat of the tub, shamelessly watching as a few scattered rose petals slid down the ripples of his torso, when he climbed out of the tub.

He walked over to grab us each a towel from one of the drawers. The towels were made of that same soft, thick material as the ones he had in his bathroom downstairs that I loved. After draping one of the towels around his waist, he walked over to help me out of the tub. My wet feet felt cold when they hit the marble tiling of the floor. Jasper draped the other towel he was holding around my shoulders and pulled me into his body, as he proceeded to dry me off. Our bodies melted into one another as the steam from my skin, still warm from the water, rose between us. He kissed me again and swiftly swept me off my feet. I was startled when he carried me over to the bed, like a baby in his strong, muscular arms, but his moves were more than welcome on my end. *Yes, please!* It was like we both just couldn't get enough of each other.

He planted me on the edge of the bed, nudging me to lay back. The towel had fallen at my sides, exposing the remnants of rose petals that were still pressed up against my rib cage. Jasper gently peeled one off and skated it along my skin in a feathery-like touch, trailing the petal from my navel to the center of my chest before placing it in between my breasts. My skin prickled in anticipation.

"My beautiful Angel..." He whispered as he followed the trail he'd left behind with his lips, planting soft kisses all the way up until he reached my collar bone and gave it a little nip. Droplets of water from his hair dripped onto my neck, sending tingles over my entire body as he raised his face to mine. I peered deep into the ocean of his eyes, silently begging him to kiss me. He answered my plea with his lips. Our tongues crashed into one another, as we explored our passion for each other by taste. Jasper was the first to break free.

"Wait here." He said, as he rose to his feet to grab a condom from his nightstand. The cool air hit my skin, leaving me in wait for his warmth to return. I closed my eyes and let my head fall back against the feather down comforter on his bed. For a moment, I let my mind escape into a fantasy of lying in the clouds. Jasper soon returned me to my current existence when he slid his hands up my thighs.

"Open up, Angel...I wanna taste you first..." He breathed against my knee as he spread my legs wide open. The butterflies took a dive inside my tummy at his suggestive words before swaying to the notes of the piano masterpiece that filled my ears. *And to think... This epic ride into fantasy land was only just beginning!*

My cries were incoherent when he eagerly placed his lips on me and sucked hard on the bud of my clitoris. *Did he think I was actually made of honey?* I wondered. *Who cares, this feels amazing!* Jasper was even more turned on by my body's response to him, as he slowly began to push his fingers in and out of me, like a pendulum, while continuing the dance of his tongue against my clitoris.

Just when I thought I could no longer take any more, I heard the tear of the condom wrapper. He quickly wrapped himself in it and flipped my body over, bringing my naked rear front and center to his attention.

My upper body was draped over the bed with my feet planted on the floor. He gave my ass a light smack before entering me from behind. I closed my eyes as the pressure of his fullness increased inside me. *Did he just find my favorite position?* I wondered as I cried out in pleasure when he found his way inside me. "Ahh!"

He moved in and out of me like the soft waves of the ocean in calm waters. "Jasper!" I cried out as my body rocked against his rhythm. Hearing my voice speak his name triggered his response as he increased the intensity of his motion. I quickly met him in tune. Soon we were both caught in what seemed to be an endless current of sweet ecstasy.

"Hold on, Angel" He said, while gathering my hair within his fist and gave it the slightest tug. The pressure of the pull brought even more pleasure on my end, as I turned my head to meet his face. He quickly pressed his lips to mine. Our tongues collided and began to dance as if it were choreographed by the music that magically seemed to match the passion between us.

With his free hand, he reached around me to take a pinch at my nipples that were already hardened with desire, longing to be touched. My moaning increased at the sensation when he cupped my breast while holding my hair in his hands, pulling me back against his body as he dove himself deeper inside me. My heart was pounding. I could feel the wetness of his skin against mine.

In that moment, it felt like we were no longer individuals, we were moving in unison, as if we were one. I could feel his energy inside me beginning to erupt and I knew that he was close to finding his release. He quickly withdrew his hand from my breast and reached down between my legs to claim my orgasm with a single press of his thumb on the bud of my clitoris. "Ahh" I could no longer contain the pleasure I felt inside my body. It seeped right out of me, through my voice and through my tears. Jasper fell over me, with his chest pressed against my back, I could feel his heart thumping just as fast as mine. We laid there for a few minutes catching our breath until he rolled over to the side of me.

"Come here." He said, pulling me in for another sweet kiss."I'm gonna grab a shower. I have a little something for you." He stood up from the bed and went inside his closet to grab a beautiful wrapped sweater sized gift box.

"You didn't have to buy me anything." I protested.

"I know I didn't have to, I wanted to. Just open it and put it on. I won't be long." He said before leaving me with the gift.

I waited until Jasper was no longer in sight to open up my gift. The gift was wrapped so beautifully, I didn't want to mess up the pretty paper. I slid my finger along the sides where the tape was, trying my best not to tear up the packaging. Even the box looked exquisite. I could only imagine what may have been inside it.

It was white with light pink polka dots and felt velvety in its texture. It had a large black ribbon tied around it with a key attached to the end. I was curious as to what the key was for. I tugged at the ribbon to release it from the box and set the key aside on the dresser until I could ask him about it. Beneath the white tissue paper, I discovered a long metallic colored lavender gown with spaghetti straps that felt like it was made of pure silk. Tucked inside the box, I found even more tissue

11

paper. I removed the tissue paper to reveal a black colored kimono style robe that was made of the same fabric. I couldn't believe it! The gown was a perfect match to my bra and panty set I had splurged on at Victoria Secrets a few years back, right before I met AJ. I had worn the set the night that Jasper and I first made love. *He must have remembered.*

I seriously wanted to pinch myself! *Could this night get any better?* I wondered as I slipped into the gorgeous gown. I walked over to the full length mirror that stood in the corner of the room by the window to see how it fit. The gown suited my body like a glove, hugging my curves in all the right places. The top of the gown was trimmed in a double layer of soft black lace that covered my breast and the lavender silk material flowed down from my rib cage, falling just above my knees. I could swear I had never worn anything that felt so soft. So luxurious. Jasper's jaw dropped in his reflection, when he came out of the shower and stood behind me in his towel.

"You look stunning, Angel. I just couldn't resist when I came across it. This gown was made for you, just like you were made for me." Jasper said, smiling to himself, as he spoke his thoughts out loud. "Well, do you like it?" He asked.

I turned around to face him. "I love it! Thank you, Jasper!" I replied with a kiss to his cheek where his dimple was proudly staring back at me.. "What's the key for?" I asked in a curious tone as I picked it up off the dresser and held it up for him to see.

Jasper smiled wide. "That's *your* key to the lake house. I'm going to take you to see it tomorrow." He replied. "That is, if you don't have any other plans, of course." *Seriously?! He's kidding, right?* I was so surprised that he would actually give me the key to his new property.

"You're my plans… now that you're here with me." I said, returning his smile with my own. "Thank you so much for coming to my party. I know it wasn't easy for you to be here, I appreciate it. More than you know."

Chapter 3

⚜

After another round of what some might call sinful pleasure, Jasper and I both slept soundly wrapped in the comfort of each other's arms. My heart was so full of joy from all the love I had received from all my new friends. The gift of Jasper's presence was the only thing missing to unlock my heart. And Boy! Did he come in, like a knight in shining armor, to quite literally hand me the key?

When the wee hours of morning seeped in through the cracks of the curtain, I awoke feeling so happy that I could burst. My cup was overflowing. I wanted to do something to show my love and gratitude for Jasper in return. So I did what I did best!

I slipped out from underneath the covers, as quietly as possible. I didn't want to wake him until everything was ready. I stood at the corner of his bed, watching his chest rise and fall. He looked so peaceful and content. Inhaling a breath of gratitude for all that he was, I quietly slipped out of the bedroom, closing the door behind me. I didn't want Lucas to wake him up when he saw me.

I closed the other door to the bathroom for an extra padding of silence, hoping Jasper would sleep in. Just like his daddy, Lucas was snoozing away in his crate, with all four paws up in the air. It was hard not laugh at the sight before me as I passed by the giant snoring pup. I tucked the key that Jasper gave me into the outside pocket of my overnight bag and went downstairs to brush my teeth and get dressed in the guest bathroom.

I threw on a pair of faded denim jeans and a black cami top, opting to leave the sweater I brought in case it got cold inside my bag for now. I gave my cheeks a pinch and went into the kitchen to cook breakfast for Jasper. I wanted to thank him for showing up for me. *In more ways than one.*

I opened up the fridge to see what I was working with. *BINGO!* Eggs were definitely on the menu! I was honestly surprised at how well stocked his fridge was for being a bachelor. Clearly, he took his health seriously.

I pulled the carton of eggs out of the fridge and set them out on the kitchen island counter. I didn't see any bacon, but he did have some vanilla Greek yogurt and plenty of berries. *I know... I could make us some parfaits!* The bushel of spinach and carton of mushrooms also caught my eye, so I pulled them out as well.

When I opened up the pantry to see what else was on hand, I found a loaf of bread. It wasn't the traditional white bread I was used to, it had all sorts of nuts and seeds. I certainly wasn't opposed to giving it a try, so I pulled that out too. My eyes roamed the shelves and settled on the box of granola bars on the very top shelf, figuring it would make the perfect addition to our parfaits! All I had to do was crush them up and sprinkle them on top.

With everything laid out on the kitchen island, I settled on a menu. Mushroom and Spinach Omelet and toast with Berry Yogurt Parfaits. Considering the fact that all the ingredients were literally chosen by Jasper when he bought his groceries, I could only hope he would like what I had planned. I put on a pot of coffee and began searching the cabinets for a frying pan when I heard shuffling coming in from the loft upstairs. Lucas's cries became louder and soon after, he and Jasper were making their way down the stairs. *Shit!* I really wanted to have it all ready for him before he woke up.

Lucas was the first to greet me in the kitchen where I embarrassingly stood in front of the kitchen island with all the ingredients laid out for the breakfast I had planned to make. Jasper trailed in behind him, scratching his head. He was dressed in yet another pair of baggy gray sweatpants and a loose fitting white tee shirt. *Damn! Does this man ever not look sexy?!* I wondered. Even with his bed head, and sleepy eyes, all I could think about were the images flashing through my mind of the night before.

"I thought I smelled coffee." The early morning, scruffy tone was prominent in his voice." What's all this?" He asked, teasing me with that dimple in his smile.

Caught in the act, I was feeling bashful about my plans to take over his kitchen without asking. "Um... Breakfast? I was just looking for a frying pan for the eggs." I replied, coyly.

"You're adorable when you squirm, Angel. Don't be shy... I told you to make yourself at home. Breakfast sounds fantastic!" We heard the perk of the coffee maker alerting us that it was ready. Jasper grabbed a mug from the cabinet above my head and poured himself a steamy cup of Joe. All I could do was stand there staring with a stupid grin on my face like some goofy teenager with her crush.

Lucas nudged Jasper's hand and let out a whine. "I'd better take him out." Jasper said.

"Great!" I said. "Everything should be ready when you two get back!" I said, happy to have him out of my hair. He was far too distracting for me to actually carry out my plans with him in here. Jasper grabbed the frying pan I had been looking for and placed it on the stove, gave me a quick peck on the lips before he and Lucas took off for their morning jog.

I set the table with our plates of food and went back to the kitchen to pour us each a glass of orange juice when I heard the elevator ding. Jasper and Lucas returned from their walk. Lucas made a beeline for his water dish and Jasper set his leash on the kitchen island.

"Everything is ready," I said, pointing to the dining room table. "I just have to grab us some silverware. Please have a seat."

"You sure you don't need any help?" Jasper asked as he took a seat at the dining room table. His white tee shirt now had sweat stains from his run.

"Nope, I got this!" I said, placing his glass of orange juice in front of him. I returned to the kitchen to grab my own glass orange juice and our silverware. When I opened up the silverware drawer, my glass of orange juice hit the marble floor and shattered into a million pieces.

I was caught off guard by what I found sitting right on top of the silverware rack inside the drawer. A photograph of an ultrasound. On the lower white portion of the photograph read the words: "Where did you go, Daddy?"

Jasper quickly jumped up and ran over to me in the kitchen to see if I was alright. By the time he reached me, my eyes were already filled with tears and I could feel all the blood rushing to my cheeks. I could barely breathe as all the pieces of the puzzle had finally fit into place at the mere sight of what was in my hand. I held it out to him and he took it from my hands.

I had no words. I never could speak when my emotions ran through me like a wildfire. The look on Jasper's face when he saw my reaction to the photo confirmed everything I needed to know. It was all in plain sight in front of me the whole time! *How could I be so blind?* All the clues were there the night of Sam's birthday dinner! This was the secret he had been hiding from me all along. *And what about Sam? That was his best friend! How could he do this?* It was all so far beyond my realm of understanding. I couldn't just stand there crying in front of him. I had to get out!

I swiped up my bag and ran towards the elevator, jabbing at the buttons as if I were trying to escape a masked murderer. Jasper didn't even run after me because *he knew.* He knew just how hurt I was. I felt like such a fool. I should have known it was all too good to be true. *Jasper was too perfect! How could he lie to me this whole time? Why, of all people, did he have to choose me?* After everything I had been through, this was the last thing I needed to be a part of.

When the elevator that seemed to take forever finally came, I stepped inside and took one last look at Jasper who was now standing in front of it, saying absolutely nothing. He just stared at me, with a sad puppy dog look on his face and said nothing. I was thankful when the elevator doors closed.

Chapter 4

⌒⊶⊷⌒

Jasper

I always knew that something wasn't right with Sam's girlfriend, Lena. It kinda felt like a punch in the gut when he told me how he'd met her. She solicited herself to him at a high stakes poker game in one of the underground casinos in New York. Sam, being the gambler that he was, pushed all in. It shouldn't surprise me that she was now claiming me as the father of her unborn child and trying to blackmail me to keep her from having an abortion. A child that Sam truly believed was his!

A few months back, I woke up with Lena in her and Sam's bed, with no recollection of had how I'd gotten there. I may have had a reputation for being promiscuous… looking for love in all the wrong places, but I always wore a condom and could never do that to my best friend. Especially knowing just how much he loved her! *How ironic is it that one night of sex that I couldn't even remember would somehow lead to an unplanned pregnancy?* It was just my luck. I figured I was black out drunk, but I had done away with that sort of behavior a long time ago.

She tried to make me stay, but I got out of there quick, before Sam might come and find me. I was so repulsed, I didn't even say a word to her before I left that morning.

When I came home from my new lake house property to get ready for Carla's party, I found at least a hundred of those damn sonogram photographs plastered all over my penthouse. I thought I'd gotten rid of them all. I even called down to security, right away to change my pin code. How could I not believe she would be devious enough to stash some away where I might not find them. She totally set me up!

My world shattered the instant I saw the look on Carla's face. It was one that would honestly tear my beating heart right out of my chest. I never wanted to hurt her. It was my plan to tell her everything, when I took her to the lake house. I had hoped that after painting a picture of what I hoped our future could look like, she might find it in her heart to try and understand the situation. I knew it was a long shot. I never expected her to truly understand, but I was hoping that she might.

All I really wanted was to see her happy for just one weekend before I would ultimately let the chips fall wherever they landed. Being honest was my only fighting chance at keeping her. Now, she knew everything. Well, she knew enough, at least, to know I had kept this giant secret from her. And now she felt betrayed. I could see it in her eyes when she looked up at me. The sadness.

How could I be so stupid, letting her find out this way? If only I had chosen to man up when she needed me to. I would never be left with the memory of the expression on her face when she took her things and left me. I didn't even have the chance to explain.

Maybe I didn't deserve her in the first place. After all, *she* was perfect! Why would I even think I was worthy enough to have her as mine? Worthy or not, I knew I wouldn't let her go without a fight, even if it took my last breath! Even if I had to wait, I would be there for her when she was ready. If that time would ever come. At this point, I could only hope it might.

Carla

How a girl could go from being the happiest in the world to being the saddest in a day's time was beyond me. After my party, Jasper and I spent the night together. Our night of passion was like the icing to my belated birthday cake. We were both longing for each other so badly, that our passion for one another had swallowed us both up into our own little cocoon of ecstasy. We spent half the night in bed together, making love. It was like we were in our own little world. Nothing else existed but the heat of the fire that raged on between us.

Little did I know that today would bring me news that would not only devastatingly shatter the magnetic force field we had been surrounded by since we'd met, but also drive a perfect storm of chaos, full of harsh realities, to destroy us.

I felt like such an idiot to have the truth staring back at me the entire time. Every clue was plain as day, but I was so blinded by my hope in sharing what I thought I truly deserved with Jasper. A love that made me feel whole. To love and be loved in return. How could I let my guard down and be so naive. *Hadn't I learned my lesson with AJ?* Maybe I just didn't want to believe that the world was only full of men who lied.

The only man I'd ever met who was ever honest and true, was Joel, my stepfather. He'd given Mama everything she'd ever wanted in a marriage and that left me with enough faith to believe that Jasper could do the same for me.

When I got back to Jamie's apartment, her and Dillon were still sleeping. It was barely 8 o'clock. I was honestly relieved that I could process everything in my own time without having to explain everything. The truth was, I was really falling for Jasper. *Hard.* I just couldn't understand it. Everything else he was to me had painted him in such a different light. He was caring and kind. He was a true gentleman when it came to me, every step of the way. Even with how he handled meeting Mama and Abby. It just didn't make any sense that this could be the same person who would cheat on me with his best friend's fiance and hide the fact that he would soon be the father to her unborn child. I wondered for a moment how Sam would feel when he, too, found out the truth.

I channeled into the memory of Sam's birthday dinner to try and gain some more insight of the situation. It was a night I had tried to forget in an attempt to sweep my nagging feelings under a rug. My intuition tried to warn me, once again, I refused to listen. I wanted so desperately for the vision I had of Jasper to remain intact. The signs were all there pointing to the truth. Jasper was so uneasy in their company. I just sat there, letting myself sink into the news of their new coming child and what that would typically mean for a couple. With that, I had cast away everything my gut was telling me about the energy I was feeling at the table.

Sam seemed a lot friendlier than Lena. He exuded an energy of warmth, but I still had the sense that he couldn't be trusted. There was something dark lurking beyond the surface. Whatever it was, he didn't appear to be consumed by it. At least, not yet. With Lena, all I could feel was her darkness. She was as cold as the Antarctic Sea.

It was clear now why Jasper was so angry with her. She was trying to get a rise out of him. Drinking her wine in his face, knowing fully well that she was pregnant with his child. I was beginning to feel sick to my stomach just thinking about how evil that was. But like any darkness I had ever come into contact with, my curious nature wanted to understand what was lying beneath the surface to bring them to it.

Between channeling into the memory of Sam's birthday dinner and all of these unprocessed emotions that were consuming me, the lighthearted energy I woke up with this morning in Jasper's bed, was now a distant memory. I felt exhausted and drained and my appetite had completely vanished. I quietly slipped into my bedroom, so I wouldn't wake Jamie and Dillon. I climbed into bed without even changing my clothes and let the tears fall until I fell asleep.

Chapter 5

I 'm lying in bed, but it's not my own. My eyes are closed and everything is quiet. Suddenly, I can feel fingertips tracing over my temples, coaxing me to open my eyes, but something inside me is afraid to see who it is.

One of the fingertips slowly begins to travel down my face to trace over my lips, down my neck to where my collar bones meet, then turns back up to my lips again, where they gently begin to pry them open. As the single fingertip roams around inside my mouth, I am surprisingly delighted by the taste, sweet like caramel.

Reluctantly, I allow my eyes to flutter open, finding Jasper's deep blue eyes as they peer back at me. There's a sense of safety now blanketing over my initial gut feeling of fear. His face is surrounded by a strange, but welcoming halo glow that lures me in to kiss his lips. Soon our tongues begin to reacquaint with each other as if they'd both been lost and longing for each other for a thousand lifetimes.

This is no ordinary kiss. In fact, there is enough heat in this exchange to melt a thousand glaciers. I am aroused beyond measure and can't help my eyes from closing again. All of my senses are intensely engaged in the moment. My tongue feels like its on fire, but I just can't seem to let myself break free from his lips.

Soon, the fire between us becomes more intense than ever. I can literally smell the smoke in the air. I open my eyes again to find the entire room that we are in is now smoldering, and a blazing fire is beginning to consume the bed where we lay.

"Jasper" I cry out, but it's already too late. I can no longer see him in front of me as the fire dissipates, like magic, just as fast as it came in. The fire has already consumed his entire body, until all that I am left with are the ashes of his remains. "Noooo!"

"Carla, honey! Wake up!" Jamie cried, nudging at my shoulder. "You're having another nightmare."

"Jasper!" I cried out again. My mind was caught somewhere between the realm of sleep and my current reality. My eyes flutter open to see Jamie with a look of deep concern on her face.

"Jamie?" I asked, in a tone of confusion, as I gathered my thoughts to my surroundings. A world I didn't even want to be in right now. A world, where the truth had completely tarnished any possibility of a future to exist between Jasper and me. My eyes suddenly began to fill with tears as I suddenly recalled what transpired earlier that morning. "Oh, Jamie." I sobbed.

"What's the matter, sweetie?" She asked. "Are you alright?"

26

"No... It's over." I choke the words out between sobs.

"What do you mean? What's over?" Jamie couldn't understand why I was upset.

"Jasper... He's seeing someone else." I managed to get out. Jamie's face fell at my words.

"What?! You're kidding, right? There's no way! Are you sure?! That doesn't make any sense! It was just a dream..." She sounded hopeful in her assumption. She thought I hadn't fully come to my senses from whatever it was that I was dreaming about.

"No, it's true. He's...." the tears began to pour down my face like a faucet. "He's..."

"He's what?" Jamie asked, impatiently waiting for a greater understanding of the situation.

"He's.... He's having a baby." I finally spit the words out.

"A baby?" She asked with a scrunch between her eyebrows. "Having a baby? With who?!"

"With Lena!" I replied as I turned my head back into the pillows so she couldn't see my face. Watching her react to my sadness was only making me cry even more.

"Lena? Who is Lena?!" Jamie asked. "I'll kill him, I swear!" I heard her mumble under her breath.

"Lena! She's Sam's girlfriend." I shouted through the pillows, as if Jamie knew who I was talking about. Suddenly it dawned on me that I hadn't exactly told her who Lena was or anything about what happened that night at Sam's birthday dinner.

"Who is Sam? Jasper's friend, the co-owner of Club Hush?" Jamie asked as she tried to piece the puzzle together.

I pulled my head up to look at Jamie. "Lena is 'Blonde Bimbo'!" I shouted before crashing back down into the pillows. Jamie instantly began rubbing my back.

"I'm ready. Maybe we can catch them before they stop making breakfast." Dillon called in through the doorway, completely in the dark from what was happening.

"Just give me a sec!" Jamie replied. "Carla's here, and she needs me." Jamie called back to Dillon.

"Don't worry about me, I'll be fine, Jamie. Please don't mess up your plans." I said, wiping the tears from out of my eyes. Jamie looked at me and back at Dillon, as the wheels began to spin in her mind.

"I know… Why don't you come with us? We can wait. I'm sure we can still make breakfast too, if we hurry. Besides, Breana and Ryan are meeting us there, we can probably call in our orders to them on the way." Jamie asked, sounding hopeful I might agree.

"I appreciate that, but I'm really not hungry. I'd really like to just stay here." I replied with a small smile to let her know I would be okay. With all the practice I had, I was a master at playing pretend.

"Are you sure?" Jamie asked, still trying to convince me. "I hate to leave you here like this."

"No, really, I'm good. Go have fun and enjoy your time with Dillon, while he's here." I replied.

"Okay," Jamie said, exhaling to the sound of defeat. She reached over and gave me a big hug. "Get some rest. And promise me you'll eat something. All that crying will deflate your energy."

"Promise!" I said.

"Pinky Promise?" She asked again, extending her pinky finger out to me.

"Pinky promise!" I said, looping my finger through hers.

"Okay, we'll talk more later, honey." Jamie said, reassuringly.

~

After a few hours of tossing and turning in bed, I finally decided to get up and make some coffee. As it turned out, coffee was the last thing I needed. It only made things worse. My mind would not stop racing back and forth about everything. Something seemed very off about this situation. In my mind, I wanted to forget he even existed because of how hurt I was, but my heart refused to let me.

I pulled out my new journal and began writing, attempting to gain some clarity on how I was truly feeling. I found myself longing for Jasper more than ever, despite how betrayed I felt. ***He's having a baby***

with her! *I wrote down to remind myself.* **I need to get over him! I have to let him go!**

Suddenly, I realized that I still hadn't quite wrapped my head around the severity of the situation. ***HE CHEATED ON YOU WITH HIS BEST FRIEND'S FIANCE!! LENA IS PREGNANT WITH HIS CHILD!!!!***

As I sat there, staring at the words I had written down, all the red flags were staring back at me. And yet, somehow, I still couldn't seem to get it through my thick skull. I couldn't stop thinking about him. Every time the image of his face came to surface in my mind, the butterflies would take a dive into an abyss of the loss I felt of not having him.

I hadn't realized just how strong my desire was for him, in spite of everything I knew. In a bit of frustration, I threw the pen across the bed and let out a huge sigh. I needed to get out and get some fresh air. Maybe a walk down to the park could help me clear my mind. At this point I was willing to do anything to get him off my mind.

Desperately needing some musical distraction to fill the space between my ears, I pulled out my new iPod and went on you tube to learn how to use it. I pulled up a search on as many liberating songs I could find and loaded them all onto my iPod to take with me on my walk. I was determined to get over Jasper, more than ever!

Chapter 6

The task of loading my iPod took a little while, but it kept me busy. Each song took a few minutes to download and by the time I was finished, I had every song I could think of that might empower me in moving on from Jasper.

I stepped outside to a crystal clear, blue sky above. The air felt cool against my skin when the breeze picked up. The sun was in its final hour before the sky would turn to dusk. I snuggled my earbuds into my ears and tuned the rest of the world out with the sound of the songs I needed to let my heart hear. With every passing face, I gave a nod in acknowledgment, but I couldn't seem to form a single smile to exchange.

Walking to the beat, I found myself at the park in what seemed to be no time at all. The hot dog vendor was packing up his stand for the night and the lady who fed the ducks was parked at her usual spot on the bench. I took a seat on the bench across from her, so I could watch as all the ducks line up for a chance to steal the bread from out of her hands.

Since you been gone, by Kelly Clarkson, was blaring through my ears. I really wanted the lyrics to resonate with me, but all I could think about was the last time that Jasper and I had come to this very spot. The night he told me he wished he could pull me behind the bushes. I felt a sudden twinge in my belly at the mere thought.

Out of nowhere, as if I brought him to life with my thoughts, guess who turned the corner on the walking trail? That's right, you guessed it! Jasper and Lucas were headed right in my direction. I couldn't tell if he noticed me or not. My first instincts were to duck behind a tree, but I knew that if I had attempted to stand, he was sure to see me. With my luck, Lucas would surely sniff me out anyway.

My heart began to beat faster, the closer they got to the bench where I was sitting. I had no idea what to say to him. Half of me was still drawn to the fire that apparently still raged on between us, and the other half never wanted to speak to him again.

We locked eyes, and I felt the sorrow pouring out of his soul. His energy felt just as defeated as mine. I quickly turned away, silently letting him know that I was in no mood to exchange any words with him. Thankfully, he took the hint and kept on running. *Phew!* By some miracle, I escaped Lucas's radar. It would have been very awkward if Lucas pounced on me with kisses, like he normally did.

When I was no longer within their range of sight, I couldn't help but watch them. I soon learned what kept Lucas at bay when he stopped to pop a squat in the grass. I felt feverish when Jasper bent over to pick up Lucas's waste. *STOP IT! You have to let him go! He's having a* baby and HE CHEATED ON YOU, for crying out loud! LET HIM GO!!!! What's wrong with me?! I wondered. I silently scolded myself for the intrusive lust that took over me. I couldn't understand why I was still magnetically attracted to someone who infuriated me at the same time. I was a complete mess! I waited long enough to ensure there wouldn't be any more awkward run ins, and went back to Jamie's apartment.

Chapter 7

When I walked through the front door, Jamie and Dillon were both in the kitchen, drinking wine. Jamie was putting her famous Tuna Casserole in the oven. I sniffed it out as soon as I walked through the door, but my appetite was still non-existent.

"Hey you!" Jamie called out when she heard me close the front door. "I'm making your favorite for dinner! It'll be ready in half an hour! Come have a glass of wine with us!" Her concern for me was evident in her invitation, but sitting down to dinner with them was the furthest thing from my mind. I was in no mood for company and I didn't want to put a damper on their night, with my pity party.

"I appreciate it, Jamie. I'm just not feeling up to it. I'm really tired, I think I'm gonna call it an early night. Perhaps you can save me a plate for lunch tomorrow?" I offered. I didn't want to be rude. I knew that she was doing all she could to try and cheer me up.

"Of course, honey." She replied, exchanging glances with Dillon. I was certain that she'd already told him what happened. I could see the concern in his expression, but he didn't say anything. Just as I expected, my mere presence was already making things weird, which was why I needed to give them their space. Dillon would only be here for the weekend, and the last thing I wanted was to be the star of their show.

I took my shoes off and headed for my bedroom. Truthfully, I wasn't really tired, I just wanted to be alone with my thoughts for a while. I set my iPod down on the nightstand, plugged in my phone to charge and got in bed. A moment later, Jamie tapped on my door before entering my bedroom.

"Hey, sweetie... Are you sure you're alright?" She asked.

"Yeah... I'm fine." I replied. "Just hurt, is all. It's been a long day. I'm more tired than anything. I think I'm just going to read for a little bit and go to bed."

"Well, that's completely understandable... No one would have ever guessed that Jasper would do this to you. It just doesn't make any sense! But I'm sure you probably don't want to think about it anymore."

"You're a great friend, Jamie. I'm really lucky to have you," I paused. "I appreciate your concern, but please... go have fun with your boyfriend. He's only here for the weekend!" I reminded her.

"Alright! Alright... Just know that I'm here if you need to talk!" She said, as she leaned in give me a hug.

"Yes, I know," I said, wiping away a tear that was threatening to break the dam. "Thank you! Now GO!" I said, shooing her away as I grabbed my book from off the nightstand and stuck my nose in it.

"OK, Okay! I'm going!" She laughed before leaving me alone in my room.

I was 3 chapters into my reading, thankfully getting lost within the story, when I heard a notification come through on my cell phone. It was a text from Jasper.

Jasper:

Listen Angel. I know you probably never want to talk to me again. Even though that breaks my heart, I completely understand. Please, whatever you do, don't give up your job at Silver Linings on account of me. Everyone there loves you and Maggie truly needs you. I promise to be gone before you begin your shift each day so you won't feel awkward. I know this job means a lot to you. You don't deserve to lose it on account of my dumb ass mistakes.

I knew I shouldn't have opened it, I was curious to see what he had the balls to say. I was a bit surprised, however, that despite our differences he was still trying to protect me. I didn't reply back. I'd be lying if I said I wasn't grateful to him to even have this job in the first place. No matter how angry I was at him, I would always be grateful to him for that.

Quite honestly, he was right. I had been wondering how to approach the situation with my job at Silver Linings. I rarely saw him there, but I was very concerned about bringing our drama into the office. Bumping into him would definitely make me uncomfortable. Especially with all of these unprocessed emotions. I stifled my urge to reply and went back to reading.

I must have fallen asleep because the next thing I knew, it was Sunday morning. Once again, Jamie tried to include me in her plans with Dillon. They were off to breakfast and a movie before Dillon had to head back to New York. I politely declined, of course. My only plans for the day, were to get some laundry and reading done.

I welcomed a day to be alone with my thoughts. I was still lost somewhere between the heartbreak of losing Jasper and why I still felt so incredibly drawn to him despite our crazy set of circumstances. I would never let on to anyone about that, though. Those were feelings I would keep to myself, because I was embarrassed by them. *How could I still have feelings for a guy who cheated on me with his best friend's girlfriend?*

And here, I thought AJ did me wrong, but somehow, this felt even worse. Jasper came into my life like my life like a hero, only to leave me high and dry. Talk about betrayal. *Would I ever be able to trust another guy again?* I seemed to be batting a thousand at this point, and I was only 24 years old. *Am I destined to be an old maid?* I wondered.

Chapter 8

There was an envelope sitting on my desk with my name on it, when I arrived at the office on Monday afternoon. It was written in Jasper's handwriting. Behind it, a vase of freshly trimmed, long stemmed, red roses. Fresh cut flowers weren't anything different from the norm, it was Jasper's way of brightening things up around here. He tended to all of the gardening of the property at Silver Linings. All of the offices had fresh cut flowers. I was fully aware of what he was trying to accomplish with these flowers in particular. I was no fool. He was trying to jog my memory of our last night together, before everything turned sour.

I quickly tossed the envelope into my purse before anyone might pass by and encourage me to open it. Whatever was inside was sure to stir me up, and that was the last thing I needed here at the office.

I went about my day as usual. I already knew getting over Jasper was going to be difficult. Especially with these little reminders of him and what we could have had if things were different. The worst part about it all, was the loss of the magic I felt inside, just knowing that we were together. And the promise of a life I had imagined with him in it. It was like my world had lost all of its color and charm. The zest had completely vanished. I felt like I was walking through life with a giant cloud over me. Even the rations of food I ate to keep my strength seemed to have no taste.

Maggie barely came out of her office, all day. She didn't let on if she knew anything about what had transpired between Jasper and me, the few times that she did. I, sure as hell, wasn't going to be the one to tell her. I was happy to keep it all a secret, because it would easier to just pretend that everything was fine. I was used to playing that card, anyway. In fact, it was beginning to feel like my leading role in life.

When I came home from work that evening, I found Jamie stretched out on the couch, working on her laptop.

"Hey Jamie." I said as I hung my keys on the hook by the door. I was trying to be more open with her. She and I had barely spoken since everything went down between Jasper and me. I'd been very reclusive. Jamie knew me well enough to respect my space and that I needed time to process everything before I could begin to open up to her about how I was feeling.

"Hey. How are you? How did everything go at work today?" She asked curiously,as she turned to face me. I wasn't the only one who considered the challenges I might face in keeping my job at Silver Linings.

"Everything went well." I replied. "Jasper wasn't there. He's usually gone before I start my shift." I could have told her about the letter he left me, but I didn't want to reveal that just yet because I hadn't even read what he wrote.

"Well, that's a relief! I was worried about that! You were so excited when you got that job, I would hate to see you quit." She said.

"Yeah…. About that!" I laughed as I took a seat next to her. "Jasper sent me a text last night."

"He did? Oh my God! What did he say?" She asked as she shut her laptop and set it on the table beside her.

"He basically said the same thing you just did. He didn't want to see me quit a job I love, over his mistakes. He also said he would ensure to be gone before my shift starts, so things won't be awkward around the office. I don't think Maggie knows, because she didn't say anything about it to me."

"How noble of him…" Jamie said, with a roll of her eyes. "Did you text him back?"

"Nope, not a word!" I said, proudly.

"Good! He doesn't deserve a response, anyway!" Jamie said, She stood up from the couch and walked into the kitchen to scope out the fridge for dinner.

"We still have plenty of Tuna casserole left, are you okay with that for dinner?" She asked, as she placed the casserole onto the stove.

"Sure, I'm gonna take a shower, real quick." I replied, as I rose to my feet.

"Okay, dinner should be ready by then." Jamie called out to me as I proceeded to retreat to my bedroom. I couldn't wait another minute to read what Jasper wrote in his letter for me. I closed my bedroom door behind me and pulled the letter out of my purse. I sat down on my bed, staring at it for a minute before finally tearing it open.

Chapter 9

Hi Angel,

This is not how I wanted to tell you this.... I know you won't understand, but the last thing I wanted to do was hurt you. I fully intended on telling you about everything when I took you out to the lake house.

Lena is pregnant, as you already know. The thing is, she swears this baby is mine. On top of that, she keeps threatening to have an abortion if I don't pay her a lot of money. Sam has no idea and I'd like to keep it that way. At least for now, until I can figure things out. He loves her so much and it would crush him if he knew.

This isn't easy to say but, the truth is... there is a possibility that Lena might be right. I woke up in bed with her a couple of months ago, but I must have blacked out from drinking. I don't understand how that could have happened because I rarely have more than a few drinks and I never really liked Lena. On top of that, as you know, I always use protection. Nothing makes sense to me about this whole situation.

I need you to know that all of this happened before I met you. I would never cheat on you. And I would never do that to Sam. He's my best friend. I'm sure you probably never want to see me again. Honestly, I can't even blame you for that.

If this baby is mine, I will not abandon it. It will be my child, and I will be the best Dad I can possibly be. The father I never had a chance to know. I have absolutely no intentions on ever being with Lena, but I will take care of her if she truly is the mother of my child.

I want you to know that my heart still beats for you and I will wait as long as I have to if I ever get lucky enough to have you stand with me in this difficult situation.

I love you. I will always love you. None of this changes that. You deserve to know the truth, no matter how uncomfortable that makes me feel. You always did. I just didn't know how to tell you all of this without hurting you in the process. Please believe me when I say, hurting you was the last thing I wanted to do.

With all my heart,

Jasper

Wait... what?! I *was* completely dumbfounded. His confession in the letter brought so much clarity to every question I had about that night at Sam's birthday dinner. *Why couldn't he have just told me all of this that night?* That would have been the right thing to do. I had to give him respect for being open about it now.

Objectively, I could understand that he may have needed some time to process everything first, just as I do when I'm faced with a difficult decision to make. *Of course, he was protecting me!* He'd never been any other way with me. It all lined up with his character. *Maybe Jasper wasn't the asshole I desperately tried to paint him into these past few days, after all.*

I folded the letter up and put it back inside the envelope before slipping it inside the top drawer of the nightstand and went inside to bathroom to shower.

~

I turned on the shower and climbed into the tub, completely lost in thought, as the warmth of the water cascaded over me. Taking on the idea of walking through a life with Jasper and a baby did seem overwhelming. It was a lot to take in. Not to mention, having Lena in our lives to constantly cause drama. It all seemed like too much for me, especially while trying to process and heal from my own trauma.

Drunk or not, sleeping with his best friend's girlfriend really gave me the creeps. I didn't think I would ever be able to just let that go. Still I would be respectful enough to keep his secret from Sam and everyone at the office. He was respectful enough to open up and give me the truth of the matter. I would, in return, give him that respect. Jasper wasn't the only guy out there in the world, maybe we just weren't meant for each other, as it had once seemed. Maybe this situation was the universe telling me to take a break and give myself more time to heal before diving head first into another relationship.

I turned off the shower and got out of the tub with a clear mind and feeling liberated. The air felt cool against my skin when I stepped out onto the rug. I don't know how long I had been in the shower, but I was sure that Jamie probably had dinner waiting and I didn't want it to get cold. After drying myself off with a towel, I hung it to dry on the bar. I slipped into my comfy robe and slippers and went out into the living room.

Jamie was setting the table for us. She poured us each a glass of white zinfandel to have with dinner.

"Hey. Feel better?" She asked, taking her seat at the dining room table.

"Much better." I replied. "This smells fantastic! Thank you," I said, surprised that my appetite was finally making its debut.

"How was your day?" She asked me again. I thought it was odd, she seemed a bit anxious. Like something was on her mind that she was trying to forget.

"It was fine. How was yours?" I asked, curiously, stealing a bite from my plate. I washed it down with a sip of wine, letting the flavors of the casserole pique the palette of my tongue.

Jamie was hesitant in her response, which told me something was definitely up with her. She seemed bothered by something. I was determined to find out what it was. "It was... good." She hesitantly replied before taking a fairly large sip of her wine. It seemed as though she were trying hard not to say what was truly on her mind. She studied me as I took my next bite as if I were a subject in some bio lab experiment. *Why is she tip-toeing around me?* It wasn't like her to keep things quiet. She had always been the type to just say whatever was on her mind.

"Spit it out, Jamie! What's up?" I asked.

"Oh. Well…." She paused and took another sip of her wine. "I just know that you're going through a lot. I don't want to bother you with something I may be deluding myself with."

"Seriously? I'm okay, Jamie!" I reiterated. "Now, tell me… What's going on?" Jamie let out a deflated sigh, as if she were a balloon I popped with a sewing needle. "Okay, so yesterday, when Dillon and I were at the movies, he got a phone call and stepped out of the theater. He was gone for almost half the movie. And when he came back, he didn't say anything to me about where he'd been." She started.

"Really?" I asked, hoping she would give me more details.

"I don't know… He was quiet before he left for New York. Too quiet. Somethings up with him, I just know it. He hasn't texted me back all day, either. Only once this morning, which really isn't like him." Jamie replied. Although she was clearly still concerned about her relationship with Dillon, I could visibly see the tension melt away from her face just to get it all off her chest. I found it funny how different we were when it came to matters of the heart. We were so opposite in that way.

"I see. Maybe something's up with him, but what do you think it could be? And why was that so hard to tell me?" I wondered out loud.

"Well, you never came out of your room last night, and I know you haven't been eating well since the incident with Jasper. I didn't want to upset you any further. Honestly, I'm ecstatic to see you actually have an appetite!" She laughed. "I don't know… I just worry about you, that's all." Jamie had a fair point. I felt terrible for making her feel like she couldn't come to me about something that was upsetting her. I had been so stuck in my own little world of self pity to notice that she needed me too.

"I'm so sorry," I started to say.

"Don't be." Jamie interrupted me. "You just had your heart broken. You're allowed to process that however you need to. I just want to make sure you're taking good care of your health, while you do it. I would be devastated if anything were to ever happen to you. You're my best friend."

"I know that, Jamie, I would be too, if anything were to ever happen to you. But the world doesn't revolve around me and my drama, that doesn't seem to want to let go of me, lately." I laughed.

"Well, at least you can laugh about it now. That's a step in the right direction." I wanted to tell her about the letter, but I wasn't quite ready. I needed time to sit with my feelings about everything before I would know how to proceed with Jasper.

"That's true." I agreed. "Maybe Dillon is just busy with work or something, he'll come around. At least you know he made it to New York, this time."

"Yeah, I hope so." She agreed.

After dinner, Jamie and I made plans for another spa day on Saturday. My nails were all chewed off now and desperately needing some love. We sat on the couch and watched movies together for the rest of the night until we both zonked out. I think we both just needed to know that we were there for one another, regardless of what the men in our lives were doing. When she got up to use the bathroom, she tapped me on the shoulder to tell me to go to bed.

Chapter 10

The coffee shop was oddly slow for a Tuesday morning, which gave Brooke and me plenty of time to catch up. I told her about what happened between Jasper and me and she was just as baffled as I was. I hadn't planned on telling her anything, but when she thanked me for inviting her and Jason to my "epic birthday party", as she called it, everything just came pouring out of me like Niagara falls.

Brooke was always so easy to talk to. Jamie was my ride or die. You know, the type of friend that wouldn't bat an eye if I'd asked her to help me hide a body, but she was so protective of me, that she was always quick to jump the gun. Whereas with Brooke, she was more like the friend that would help me mull over all the details of a situation without any judgment. Both friends were special to me, each in their own unique ways.

"That's crazy! That's that Lena girl who was here the other day, right?" She asked.

"Yes! She really is crazy! You should have seen the look she gave Jasper while she sat there, drinking her wine in his face, at Sam's birthday dinner. Pure evil!" I said, before proceeding to share with her the details from Jasper's letter.

"Well it sure seems like you're in quite the pickle jar." Brooke said, as she passed me the tray of empty sugar caddies to fill. We were using the extra time we had to get a head start on our closing side work. "That man I met at your party loves you. There's no doubt about that, but it sure sounds to me like he's got quite a mess on his hands." She said, with a raise of her eyebrows.

"Yeah, I know." I agreed. "And the worst part is... I still get butterflies, every time I think about him. I'm a mess!"

"The weird thing is, I could get over the fact that he's gonna be a father." I said, while handing the tray back to Brooke. She put it on the shelf above her head. "It's the idea of having Lena in our life that terrifies me. That woman is crazy! I think it's better if just stay far away from this whole mess. There's been so much drama in my life. Honestly, I'm just kinda over it all."

"That's understandable. Maybe you just need time to let things settle a bit." Brooke said in an attempt to console me. "At least you won't have to leave your new job. That was nice of him to give you your space. He seems to care a lot about you." She said. It was obvious to me which side of the fence Brooke was on. Clearly, she was a fan of Jasper, but she also understood how difficult the situation was.

"I don't know. I guess time will tell, for sure." I said.

"Did you see that they're having an Open Mic Night here, tomorrow?" Brooke asked, eyeing the stack of fliers on the counter by the register. "Jason and I are thinking about going. You wanna come?" She asked.

"Really? That actually sounds like fun. What time does it start?" I asked.

"It starts at 7 o'clock." She replied, as she walked over to the register to grab a flier to show me.

"Well, I do have to work, but I could come by afterwards, around 7:30 if that's OK?" I asked.

"Sure, we'll be here anyway. It says it's till 10 pm, so you'll still have plenty of time to catch the show. Jason is gonna play one of his songs and I'm gonna sing." Brooke sounded excited.

"Wow, now I'm excited! You never told me you could sing... You really blew everyone away at my party. We were all impressed! I love to sing, too. That's why Jamie got me the karaoke machine for my birthday. I just have trouble getting past my stage fright, as you probably saw." I laughed at the memory.

"You did great! I barely noticed your stage fright when you sang your song to Jasper." Brooke's eyes lit up. "I know... You said you write poems, right? Maybe you can bring some of your poetry with you. It should be a little easier than singing."

"Oh... I don't know, that brings a whole new type of vulnerability to the table." I laughed. Brooke's disappointment was evident in her sigh. "I'll tell you what... I'll bring a few with me and think about it."

51

Brooke smiled. "Deal!" She said.

A line began to form as soon as Ben walked through the door. I helped out with the rush before I took my break. Since it was a nice day out, I took my breakfast over to the park. When I returned from my break, Brooke told me that a courier had come to deliver me flowers. Ben was holding them in his office for me, until I got off work. My first guess was that they were from Jasper, but with the way things were going for me lately, anything was possible.

"Did you see what type of flowers they were?" I asked, curiously. I was still feeling a little paranoid about everything.

"Yes! They were roses. Red roses with baby's breath! At least 2 dozen!" She replied. *Phew! OK, definitely Jasper!* Yet another attempt at reminding me of the last night we spent together. It really was a beautiful ending to a perfect night. I had to give him credit for his effort. I batted down the butterflies that arose while pondering the memory. Well, his mission was accomplished.

My heart wanted to remain in the memory of the night before everything turned to shit between us. My head knew I needed to be strong and stand firm in my decision to let him go. Having to deal with Lena was just too much for me to handle, especially after everything that went down with AJ.

What I really needed was to focus on myself and rebuild my life without any crazies in it. I hated that I had to let him go. Jasper was just too good to be true. Even though my heart was grieving the loss of everything I had imagined with him, I knew my friends would ultimately be there to lift me up again. Eventually, I would feel whole again. At least I had hoped I would.

Chapter 11

L ater that night, Jamie's eyes lit up when she saw me walk through the door with my roses. "OMG! Don't tell me you have another secret admirer! Those are gorgeous!"

"Well, I'm pretty sure they are from Jasper, but let's open the card and see." I said, as I placed the vase on the dining room table. I took the card over to the sofa with me to sit in the living room with Jamie.

"I don't understand... Do you really think he would do that after everything that's happened?" She asked with a raise of her eyebrows. It dawned on me then that Jamie still didn't have a full scope of what was truly going on.

"Yeah…. About that!" I said, with a sneaky grin. "I have something to tell you, actually. But let me read the card first." I realized I had a confession to make with Jamie about the letter Jasper left me at the office. Now that I'd hinted at something, there was no way she'd let me get away with keeping it from her.

I hope you like roses, Angel. I know you probably still don't want to talk to me, but I wanted you to have my new phone number in case you need me or decide to change your mind. 617-555-9625

P.S. I can't stop thinking about you.

You have my heart, Always.

Jasper

"I don't get it! Why would he send you flowers? He has to know how bad he fucked things up for the two of you." She said, defensively. God bless her heart for trying to protect me.

"Hold on…" I said as I went to get Jasper's letter from the nightstand in my bedroom. I came back to the living room and handed it to Jamie so she could read what he wrote. I sat down on the couch and watched her scan the letter, waiting to hear what she might say in response.

"Wait… Are you kidding me?" She asked me with her eyes wide.

"I found it on my desk at work yesterday." I replied. "I was waiting to see how I felt about the situation before I showed it to you." I took a deep breath before continuing. "I don't know, Jamie. I can handle a baby… Well, at least I think I can handle a baby…. But I can't handle having Lena in our lives forever. She's certified crazy!"

"Well, that's understandable…" Jamie's eyes shot up to the left, "and also ironic. I actually have some news to tell you too."

"Oh yeah? What's up?" I asked, my curiosity piqued.

"So you remember how I told you that Dillon wasn't calling me back yesterday?"

"Yeah..."

"Well, that phone call he stepped out of the movie theater for, was his ex, Theresa. Apparently his daughter has strep throat." Jamie paused, awaiting my reaction.

"His daughter? Holy Cow! He's married?" I asked.

"No, he's not married." Jamie laughed. "They were together for a couple of years and split up just before she learned that she was pregnant. I guess they got back together for the sake of the baby a few months later. It didn't take them long to decide they were better off as friends. His daughter's name is Emily, She's 6."

"Wow... I can't believe he was keeping that from you this whole time." I said. I was dumbfounded at how the men in our lives seemed quick to lie to cover up their shit.

"Well, he said he hasn't had much luck with dating and wanted to give me a chance to get to know *him* before I passed judgment on the fact that he has a kid... Which honestly, I can understand. I just wish he would have told me sooner."

"Well, I guess I could understand his reasoning. That just makes trusting him that much harder, though, right?" I asked, silently passing my own judgment.

"He was actually very open about everything once he let the cat out of the bag. Or, daughter, rather." She laughed."Honestly, I'm excited to meet her. He wants to wait a little while longer before he introduces us to each other, which I can totally respect."

"Well, that explains a lot. I wonder if that was what made him go MIA the first time." I said, speaking my suspicions out loud.

"I'll bet it is!" Jamie said. "Do you think it could have been Lena who wrote that on your car?"

"I'm surprised that thought hasn't crossed my mind. It probably was her! I told you, she's crazy!" I replied.

"So what are you gonna do about Jasper now?" She asked. "He's clearly head over heels about you, and I know you love him...I saw the way the two of you sang to each other at your party. We all saw it!" Well that makes two for two on the Jasper scale. Both Brooke and Jamie seemed to be on 'Team Jasper'.

"I think I just need a break for now. Honestly, it's all a little too much. I've already had enough crazy with AGE." I said, trying to erase the memory of what went down with Abby. "I really *am* falling for Jasper, you're right... But with Lena added into the equation, it's just too much! That's why I think it's best to just keep my distance and try my best to get over him."

"Well, I can understand that. It's your choice." She said, as she rose to her feet. She walked over to my side of the couch and rested her hands on each of my shoulders." I'll support you, no matter what you decide to do." Jamie said before pulling me in for a hug.

"I'm gonna make a sandwich for dinner, do you want one?" She asked as she broke away from our hug.

"That sounds nice." I said. "Thank you."

"Of course, I have ton of work to catch up on, so I'm probably gonna eat in my room. The TV is all yours, tonight!" She said with a smile.

"OK, I'm gonna go grab a quick shower. Tomorrow night, dinner is on me!"

~

It felt like the TV was watching me more than anything else. My mind was lost in contemplation. It was hard to ignore the fact that both Jamie and Brooke both seemed to be on Jasper's side, even though neither of them actually came out and said so, specifically. They both wanted me to feel supported in whichever decision I chose to move forward with, regardless of how they felt about it. It was a great indicator of the value I had in their friendship. Still, I could feel where they each ultimately stood in the matter when we discussed the situation. I think my heart felt it too, but I was still on guard after dealing with AJ's shit.

I barely paid any attention to the show I was watching. After staring at the note card that came with my roses, still sitting on the side table, I decided to pick it up and plug Jasper's new number into my phone. I wanted to have it in case I ever felt called to contact him again. I couldn't help myself from wondering why he changed his number in the first place.

I knew exactly why I was keeping my distance from Jasper. I wanted to protect my heart that still couldn't seem to shake this deep attraction to him. I was beginning to feel guilty for not at least thanking him for the flowers. *What could it hurt?* I mean, it wasn't exactly his fault that his baby was being carried by the devil in human form… Having that knowledge alone, had to be difficult enough for Jasper, in itself. He deserved a thank you from me, at the very least.

After punching his new number into my phone, I hovered over the text message button for a minute thinking about what I might say.

Me:

Thank you for the letter and the flowers. They're beautiful. I really appreciate you coming clean about everything. Honestly, I do. I really wish our circumstances were different, but unfortunately, they're not. I'm afraid this is all just too much for me right now. If it were just you and this baby, it would be one thing, but we're also talking about Lena being in your life, forever. I really think I just need a break for a little while to sort things out. You've been so good to me, and I really do appreciate that. The idea of having Lena in my life sounds chaotic for me. I came here to Boston to get away from AJ and all the trauma, I don't think I can handle any more of it from Lena. I hope you can understand.

Love, Carla

I grazed my finger over the send button until I felt bold enough to press down. There it was, out there and on its way into his hands. A part of me was crying inside at how he might interpret my message. I really loved Jasper and the idea of him suffering at the expense of my words lunged at my soul like a dagger, but I still felt it was important to let him know where I stood. I turned off the TV and went to bed early.

Chapter 12

Jasper

Having control was the one thing I could always rely on that was solid. Lately, it felt like I was losing my grip on everything that mattered to me. Hell, I half wished I hadn't ever met Carla. I was in far too deep with her to only become passing strangers. She was like a wild horse, beautiful to look at, but always on the run. *And who could blame her?* My life was a mess! She deserved to be free. Free of me, and this whole situation. *How could I let myself believe I deserved to have her by my side in all of this?*

I read her text message a dozen times in bed that night. Just hearing her response was comforting because at least I knew she wasn't blaming me for what happened. It almost made things worse, because it felt like she was just beyond my reach. It was killing me that she was so close, I could almost taste her! The pain of knowing there was nothing I could do to bring her any closer was so unbearable.

Lena was standing in the way of it all, and that was beginning to drive me insane. I still had this nagging feeling that I was missing something. Something felt very off about this baby. I just felt it!

I couldn't take the endless text messages and phone calls from Lena anymore. I thought that by not answering her, she would take the hint and stop, but it only seemed to make things worse. I had to change my number for my own sanity.

Something about the night I ended up in bed with her was really getting under my skin. I remembered being so repulsed when I woke up that morning to find her lying next to me, I couldn't even fathom how I ended up there with her in the first place. But every time I would try to recall the details of that night, my mind would draw a blank.

The only time I had spent with her and Sam within the time frame of when that baby was conceived was when we were getting everything ready for the grand opening of the club. Before that, she and Sam were in NY, so I knew it had to be sometime in July or August.

The three of us would have a few drinks at the bar each night while we discussed our plans for the club. I remembered asking Tony to set up our security system right away so I could ensure everything we had inside the club would be safe, in the case of any break ins. Sam didn't think it was necessary, but he was always the more careless type, where I had always been adamant on securing my investment. *If only I could get my hands on the security footage. Perhaps I might gain some clarity on how I let myself get so drunk that night.*

It really wasn't like me at all to let myself go like that. The other thing that made no sense to me was how Sam would even leave us alone together long enough for it to happen... Despite my preceding reputation with women, I had never gave him any reason to mistrust me. He knows I would never go after someone he was with. It just wasn't like him to leave her side for very long where something like this could even happen... *Where the hell was he when all of this went down?*

Not knowing was killing me because I was the one who stood to lose the most. The amount of money Lena was asking for was pretty substantial, but nothing I couldn't get over. What bothered me the most was losing Carla in the process. Heaven help me, but the idea of handing Lena that check without fully understanding how I was the father of this child honestly made me sick. If it was truly mine, then so be it. She wouldn't have to want or need for anything ever again. Something inside me was telling me different though, and I was going to do everything in my power to find out the truth.

With all of these questions running through my mind, I could barely get to sleep. I took a shot of whiskey, to try and help me shake things off and got back into bed. Tomorrow was going to be a long day.

~

It was cold, so cold I couldn't get warm enough to sleep. The sudden sound of a baby crying quickly brought me to my feet as I crept out of bed and into the hallway to investigate. *Where was it coming from? Why did this hallway seem to go on forever?*

It was dark. I could barely see my own feet as I tracked my bare feet against the cold hard wood floor. The baby cries rang louder in my ears, the further I walked down the hall. I stopped at a

door where the cries from the baby seemed to be the loudest. The door creaked when I pushed it open.

The light of the moon shined in through the open window, as the cold winds blew its frosty breath inside the room. *No wonder why this baby was crying. It's fucking freezing in here!*

I went over to the window to close it shut. When I turned around, I noticed a lady rocking in a chair on the other side the crib, where the baby lay crying. *How could she sit here with the window wide open and let this baby cry until it froze half to death?* I wondered.

"Hello?" I called out to the woman, but she didn't respond. All she did was rock back and forth in the chair as if I hadn't even addressed her. It was too dark for me to see her face from where I stood, but her hair was light and her skin was fair. I went over to the crib to console the baby, cradling him into my arms. I held him close against my chest with one arm, while grabbing the blanket with my free hand to wrap it around him.

"How can you just sit there and neglect this baby? He could have froze to death!" I asked, in an attempt to address the woman again, but when I turned back in her direction, she was gone. What was left in her place shook me to my core. I tightened my grip on the baby and made a dash for the door.

Somehow I managed to get us both out of the room just in time, before the infestation of black snakes that were rampantly slithering across the floor could reach us. I slammed the door behind us and headed back for the room I came from.

I sat down on the bed and caught my breath as I looked down at the baby in my arms. When I found my own blue eyes staring back at me, I had to wonder if the baby was mine. The little dimple in his cheeks when he smiled gave me confirmation, but when he blinked and opened his eyes again, they turned black and stole my breath.

I woke up in a cold sweat. *It was only a dream. Thank God!* It felt so real, but I was relieved. The clock read 5:15 am when I glanced over to see what time it was. The last thing I wanted in that moment was to return to that nightmare. It was almost time for me to get up, anyway, so I went downstairs to brew some coffee. I got dressed and took Lucas out for his morning walk.

The coffee was ready, by the time we got back. I poured myself a cup and took in my morning thoughts. I had a big day planned ahead. I needed to talk to Tony about what type of access we had of the security footage history at Club Hush. I felt like I really just needed to get away from everything. The only thing keeping me here was Carla and she was pointedly, clear in her message about needing her space.

The truth was, I didn't even know if I was capable of leaving her alone, unless I were somewhere else. In order to honor her wishes, I needed to put some distance between us. Maggie could handle things at Silver Linings without me for a while. All I had to do was find a gardener to replace me while I finished the work that needed to be done on the lake house.

Chapter 13

⚜

I made sure to arrive extra early at Silver Linings, so I would have enough time to talk to Tony before work. He was stationed at the gatehouse, as usual. I parked my car around back and walked over to the gate house. I didn't want to let on about too much with him. At least not until I had more clarity on the situation with Lena. I decided to leave out the details of why I needed the footage. Tony wasn't the type to pry, anyway, so I knew I didn't have to worry about him asking me too many questions.

"Good morning. You're early today." Tony greeted me as I approached the doorway.

"Good morning. I won't be staying long today, I wanted to talk to you real quick, do you have a minute?" I asked, getting to the point.

"Sure." He replied. "Just me and the birds right now." He chuckled as he took a sip from his giant sized coffee mug. "What's up?" He asked.

66

"I was wondering if there was any way I could bring up the history of the security footage from the club. Everything is recorded, right?" I asked, trying not to sound too alarming.

"Yes. Everything is stored on the cloud. All you need is the password and pin to get on the site where it's held." He replied with a look of concern. Is everything alright?" He asked.

"Everything is fine. I just need to check on something." I replied, nonchalantly. "I'm going to be gone for a little while, at the lake house. I need to be able to check in on things, remotely. I can do that, right?" I asked.

"Of course. Let me write it down for you." He replied. He scribbled the name of the site, along with the password and pin on a notepad, then tore the page out to give to me. I folded the piece of paper and put it inside the back pocket of my jeans.

"Thanks man." I said.

"No problem. You just let me know if you need anything, alright?" Tony asked.

"You bet!" I replied. "Have a good day! And take care of the place while I'm gone, will ya?"

"Of course! That's what I'm here for!" Tony called out as I got in my car and drove up to the pair of mansions to go find Maggie.

Maggie was surprised by the news I delivered that I would be leaving again. I kept quiet about my situation with the baby. I didn't want to get her all excited. Not until I fully accepted the fact that I was the father of this child. It wasn't that I was avoiding the situation. Truth be told, I was at a point in my life where I honestly felt I was beginning to feel ready to be a Dad. With the right woman, that is. Not Lena, for Christ's sake! I wouldn't even question the situation, had it been Carla who was pregnant with my child. I gave Maggie some recommendations I had found on Yelp for a gardener and some cash to cover his work for the next few weeks, while I would be gone.

Before I left for the lake house, I left one last letter for Carla on her desk that I wrote while I was waiting for Maggie to show up to the office. I wanted her to know I was giving her the space she was asking for and to let her know where I would be in case she needed to get in touch with me for anything.

Chapter 14

⁓✦⁓

Carla

I t started raining, when I left the office. I was on my way to meet Brooke and Jason at the bookstore for our plans at Open Mic Night. I tucked the unopened letter Jasper left on my desk for me into the folder with my poems Brooke had asked me to bring, and made a dash for my car so I wouldn't get soaked.

I wasn't so sure about getting up on stage. Some of these poems held my innermost thoughts and emotions in them. It was difficult enough for me to share them with the people I loved and trusted, let alone an audience of strangers. At the very least, I would let Brooke read them herself. I hadn't known Brooke for very long, but she seemed to have proven herself trustworthy enough for me to share them with her.

When I arrived at the bookstore, I was surprised to see how crowded the place was. The store had been rearranged to allow for more seating. There was a double row of chairs all lined up in a circle. All eyes were on the center stage, where a girl with chestnut colored, fringed hair and sparkling green eyes sat on a bar stool, playing her acoustic guitar. She was singing a folk song she had likely written herself. As her beautiful voice carried through the crowd, everyone was captivated by her talent, including myself. I would be surprised if she didn't already have a record deal. I was so caught up in her song, that I nearly forgot my need to find Brooke and Jason.

I scanned the room, pushed past the crowd that stood behind the circle. I couldn't seem to find them anywhere, until Brooke came up behind me and tapped me on my shoulder.

"C'mon. We're over here. We saved you a seat! " She shouted, taking my hand to guide me through the crowd. I spotted Jason sitting on one of the couches in the background. He had his own guitar sprawled out across the couch, holding our seats. When we made it over to where he was, he stood his guitar between his legs so we could sit.

"We got here extra early to get a good seat. It's not the greatest view, but at least we can be comfortable." Brooke said as she took her seat next to Jason on the couch. I sat down next to her.

"I can't believe how crowded this place is. I've never seen so many people here before." I said, in complete awe. "That girl is really good."

"I know, right?" Brooke agreed. "She'll be a tough act to follow, that's for sure!" She laughed as she nudged her boyfriend in the arm. "Don't worry Babe, I'm sure we are gonna blow them out of the water too!"

"Thanks, Baby." Jason said, he didn't seem to worried.

The girl on stage finished her song and we all stood to applaud her performance. The host stepped up on the platform to thank the girl as she exited the stage, carrying her guitar.

"We're gonna take a short intermission. Restrooms are off to the left and the snack bar will be open for refreshments. The show will resume again in 15 minutes."

"Did you bring your poems?" Brooke turned to me to ask.

I smiled shyly. "Yes, I did actually, but you can forget about me getting up there to read them." I laughed. "I will let you read them though, if you'd like." I offered, as I pulled the dark green folder out of my bag. I swiped the envelope with Jasper's letter and put it my purse before handing the folder off to Brooke.

"I'm gonna go grab us some refreshments. Would you girls like anything?" Jason asked as he stood up from the couch.

"Grab me a coffee and something sweet!" Brooke said.

"I'll have a decaf coffee with milk and splenda, please. Thanks Jason." I replied.

"My pleasure," He said before proceeding towards the snack bar.

"Okay, let's have a look." Brooke said. She opened up the folder and began sorting through the various pages of loose leaf paper filled with my words. Some poems were written on pages that had been torn out of notebooks and a few were written in pencil and were beginning to fade from over the years.

"You really should type these out and save them in digital format." Brooke said as she sorted through the pages. She stopped to read a few and I watched a smile crawl across her face.

"This one is really sweet." She said, as she read my short poem about friendship.

"Thanks!" I said, smiling as I glanced over her shoulder to see which one she was reading. "Oh! That poem won a contest I entered in 6th grade."

"I can see why, it's a great example of how true friendship should be." Brooke agreed. She moved on to the one behind it and began reading it. Watching her react to my poetry made me realize just how much I was beginning to trust our friendship. Normally, my stomach would be tied in knots at the slightest thought of someone reading my most inner thoughts.

"This one... Wow!" She cried as she continued reading. "It's so good, Carla! It's giving Edgar Allen Poe vibes! You've really got some talent here!" As soon as she mentioned Edgar Allen Poe, I knew exactly which poem she was talking about. "You have to read this one! It's too good not to be heard!" She said, trying to convince me to change my mind about getting up on stage.

"Is it the one about addiction?" I asked, just to be sure.

"Yes!" Brooke replied.

"I don't know, Brooke... It's actually one of my favorite poems. I was hysterically, crying when I wrote it." I said, recalling just how worried

I was about AJ. He'd been gone for days and refused to answer my calls. *God only knows where he was at the time.*

Jason came back holding a tray of coffee and a brown paper bag. "I got 3 different kinds of pastries because I didn't know which one you guys would want. There's cheese danish, apple turnover and cinnamon roll. We can share all three if you want!" Jason offered.

"That sounds like fun. I'm game to share." I said, happily reverting my thoughts from painful memories to the assortment of sweet treats Jason brought back for us.

"Me too!" Brooke agreed, as she began cutting the pastries into 3 separate pieces, with a plastic knife she found inside the bag. She split the bag open to use as a make shift plate for her to work with on the small table that lay in front of the couch where we were seated. The lights dimmed as the spotlight beamed across the stage, where the host had returned to the microphone.

"Okay, next up, we have Jason Daniels and his girlfriend, Brooke who will be performing a song that Jason wrote, himself.

"That's us, Babe!" Brooke said as she quickly finished the bite of cinnamon roll she was chewing. "Let's go!" She cried, jumping to her feet. She swiped a napkin across her mouth and they were off.

I watched in anticipation as Brooke and Jason made their way through the crowd to the center of the room, where they each climbed the stairs to the platform stage. They both took a seat on the stools that were provided for them.

"This is a song I wrote for my baby." Jason said with a wink in Brooke's direction as he began strumming the strings on his guitar. Brooke sang while Jason played and when the chorus lines came through, Jason sang along with Brooke. Their melodic voices carried through the room and the entire audience was still and quiet, listening intently to the beautiful lyrics. A love song. In that moment, it was clear to me that these two were meant for each other. Their presence on stage was a true testament to the chemistry between them.

When the song was over we all stood up and applauded their performance. They both stood up from their stools and took a bow. I watched as Brooke whispered into Jason's ear. Jason turned, kissed her on the cheek and began making his way off stage, while Brooke remained front and center.

She took the microphone in her hand and began to address the audience. "This next bit, I can't take credit for. This poem was written by a good friend of mine and it needs to be shared." *Oh my God!* I was so caught up in the song, I hadn't noticed that Brooke was still holding the piece of paper with my poem in her hand. *She's gonna read it out loud!* She didn't ask me for my permission, but honestly, I didn't mind. The fact was, I just didn't think many people would even think it was very good. *As long as she doesn't point me out, I'm good.* I thought to myself as I tried my best to keep my cool.

Gone to the place
where no one has a name
Take a number, have a seat
It's time to play the devil's game
Be prepared to pay the toll

To the emptiness inside
Once you're here, you can't turn back
He will not stop the ride
Twisting and Turning
The hunger is burning
You try to stop, but you keep on returning
To the man behind the shadows
"Token Please."
The only words he seems to speak
You know it's gone, but still you reach
Empty wallet, empty pockets
No value left at all
Your walk becomes a crawl
"Please sir, I'm at your mercy."
"Token Please. You are not worthy."
Wired and tired, you walk away
As you soon begin to fade
The sun creeps above the horizon
So you find yourself some shade
To hide and reflect
A life you once knew, soon begins to blur
You've become a shell, of who you once were
Hidden behind this giant wall
You can barely even hear the call
it's coming from your phone
The one who's waiting at home
Fear of loss, fear of cost
This man has gone absurd
I try to hold him back, she says
His arms are made of steel
I try to open up his eyes

And show him what is real
Beyond my reach, it's clear, he's been taken
His soul is lost, he can't be awakened
The devil has him, he's locked in sin
All that's left, this constant need
to fill the void within

The room fell silent. *Oh my God! They hated it!* I wanted to sink into the couch, when Jason sat down next to me with his guitar. Then, all of a sudden, I watched everyone rise to their feet for a standing ovation. Someone in the crowd even whistled in the background, as the host reclaimed his spot on stage to introduce the next feature.

"Well, I think it goes without saying, your friend has got some real talent. Thank you for sharing that with us." The host said to Brooke as she stepped down from the stage to make her way back to where we were sitting. "Let's put our hands together once more for our next guest, Pete, the Puppeteer and his furry looking friend Ozzie."

"Please don't be mad at me!" Brooke cried out when she appeared in front of us with her eyes squinted and her shoulders crouched. She cautiously slid in between Jason and me as if I might hall off and hit her. "Your poem was just too good to not be shared. No one even knows it was yours." I couldn't help but giggle at her assumption of how I might react. It was definitely a bold move on her part.

"You're so silly. It's okay!" I laughed. "I honestly didn't think it would compare to the talent we've seen here. And I would never have been able to perform it the way you did, even if it were."

"Are you kidding me? Did you see the reaction from everyone? They were literally stunned! You're an amazing writer!" She reiterated.

"Okay, stop, now! You're making me blush!" I said, as my cheeks began to warm.

"It *was* really good!" Jason chimed in to back Brooke up.

"Aww, thank you, guys! You really know how to make a girl feel special. And thank you for inviting me out, this was so much fun! You guys were so good together on stage. Have you ever thought about recording an album together?" I asked, curiously.

"It's already in the works!" Brooke replied, proudly as she flashed a smile at Jason. Her confidence on stage was one to admire. "Well, Jason will be recording the album, I'm just going to be a guest on a few of the songs."

"That's so awesome. I'll be the first to buy your album, you can count on that!" I said.

There were only four acts that followed Pete's Puppeteer show, which was oddly far more entertaining that I had anticipated. After the show, Brooke and Jason walked me out to my car.

"You guys sure you don't want a ride?" I asked before opening my car door to get inside.

"Nah, It's only a few blocks down from here to Jason's apartment! Besides, we need to walk off all those pastries!" Brooke replied with a laugh.

"OK, well then, I guess I'll see you tomorrow morning. Get home safe, you two!" I called out to them as I shut the door to my car. I smiled to myself as I watched the happy couple skip off together down the street, before heading home.

Chapter 15

Jamie was already in bed when I got home. I didn't want to disturb her, so I slipped, quietly into my room and got undressed. I set my purse down on the bed and put the folder with my poems on top of the nightstand. I had such a great time with Brooke and Jason, I nearly forgot about the letter from Jasper. It felt strange, not being able to share this moment of joy with him. I sat down on the bed and let myself imagine what it would have been like if he had come with us. He would have been so proud.

I pulled the letter out of my purse and wondered what he had to say to me this time. The butterflies were beginning to stir at the mere thought of reading his words. No matter how hard I tried to fight it, I couldn't seem to get over how attracted I still was to Jasper. It was like my body completely betrayed me, whenever I would even so much as whisper his name across my mind. Still, I knew I had to let him go, regardless. I made a promise to myself, I wouldn't get too attached to whatever he might have to say in the letter before opening the seal on the envelope.

Angel,

I know you said you wanted your space and I fully intend on giving you that, if it's that's what you need. As you know, I have a lot on my mind right now and have some things I need to sort out.

Lena has been harassing me every day for this check and I honestly can't take it anymore. I almost gave it to her just to shut her up, but I know that's not the answer to all of this. She will only want more and more if I give her what she wants. It's why I had to change my number. With you needing your space and everything else I have going on, I have decided to stay at the lake house for a little while. There's still plenty of work that needs to be done and Lucas loves it there.

I wish you could come with me, but I completely understand how you feel about everything I have going on. You know how to reach me, so please don't hesitate to use my number if you need me for anything, and I mean anything at all. I miss you.

You have my heart,

Always,

Jasper

Reading his letter was difficult for me because of how it made me feel. In my heart, I wanted to stand by and support him in any way that I could. In my mind, I knew that if I had listened to my heart, I would not have learned anything from my relationship with AJ.

My heart ached for Jasper and the challenges he might face with Lena and this baby. I wish there was something I could do for him, but it was all beyond my control. All in all, Jasper really was a great guy and didn't deserve to be in the position he was in… I just knew I had to let him figure things out for himself. This whole ordeal began before I was even in the picture. I had no business being involved, especially with someone like Lena, no matter how much my heart broke for him. I laid my head back on my pillow and let my tears fall for Jasper as I fell asleep.

~

I slept right through my alarm clock the next morning. Jamie turned it off & woke me up before she left for her new yoga class. I didn't see her again until later that evening when I came home from work at Silver Linings.

I hadn't heard from Jasper all day. Even though, I knew it was for the best, I still felt a tinge of sadness. *This is what you asked for.* I reminded myself. I wondered when I would feel normal again, without having him in my life. I wasn't depressed, but my heart felt empty. Like happiness was anywhere but within me. I set my purse down on the kitchen counter and let out a sigh. Apparently it was loud enough for Jamie to hear me from the living room, where was sitting on the couch, working on her laptop.

"Hey you. How was work?" Jamie asked. "Is everything okay?" Her voice was laced in concern.

"Work was fine, thanks." I replied, trying to pick up my disposition. I didn't want to dampen her mood. "How was your day? You left early this morning." Jamie came into the kitchen where I was scouring the fridge for something to make for dinner. I wasn't very hungry, but I wanted to give Jamie a break from cooking.

"Yeah. Same old, same old. Yoga was pretty cool this morning. They have a class on Saturday. Maybe you should come! It might be good for you to release some tension, but you'll have to get up early." She laughed. I turned my head to give her a side eye.

"And just how early are we talking?" I asked.

"Listen... I know you like to sleep in, but I promise it's worth it! Class starts at 7 am." She said, still trying her best to convince me. "We can go to brunch afterwards."

"Okay." I conceded. I couldn't keep turning her down for everything she invited me to."How do you feel about tacos for dinner?" I asked.

"Sounds great! I'm starving! I'm just so busy, trying to catch up with work." She replied.

"No worries!" I said. I was happy to help *her* out for a change. "Go, finish what you're working on. I got this!"

"You sure?" She asked.

"Yes! I got this! Now go! I'll call you when it's ready!" I said, shooing her out of the kitchen.

We ate dinner together at the dining room table. Trying to escape thinking about Jasper was a challenge with the vase of sunflowers staring back at me. They were vibrant and stood high in their resilience. For Jamie's sake, I did my best to conceal my thoughts. She had a lot going on with her work and school. I didn't want to bother her with my scattered thoughts about Jasper.

"This was so good! Thank you for making us dinner." Jamie said as she cleaned her plate.

"Of course!" I said, smiling. "Don't worry about the dishes. I'll take care of it!"

"You're the best!" Jamie said as she stood up from the table. She took her laptop with her into her bedroom to finish her work.

After cleaning up the kitchen from dinner, I resorted to my own bedroom to read in hopes of distracting myself from missing Jasper. After reading the same chapter three times over without any of it processing in my head, I gave up on reading and went to bed.

Chapter 16

T he rest of the week seemed to drag along. Jasper had proven to be a man of his word and gave me the space I had asked him for. I know he was adhering to my request, but it only made me miss him more. The colorful magic I felt in knowing we were together as a couple had completely vanished. It felt like I was walking around in a world of black and white, with varying shades of gray.

When Saturday morning finally rolled around, I had hoped to feel some sort of excitement for Yoga and Brunch with Jamie, but she literally had to drag me out of bed.

"Coffee is ready! Get up!" Jamie said, cheerily.

"Okay. I'm up, I'm up!" I shouted through the blankets, but my eyes didn't want to open. Jamie turned on the lamp and pulled the blanket off me. I scowled at her.

"We're gonna be late! C'mon... I'll go make you some coffee!" She said, before leaving my room.

We barely made it to Yoga in time, before the class would begin. I was surprised at how many people were actually there, bright eyed and bushy tailed, so early on a Saturday morning. After class, we went to brunch.

We were sitting on the bench outside, watching the burnt orange shades of Autumn fall from the trees as they tumbled through the crisp cool air, when I noticed the tattoo shop across the street. I looked down at my wrist, suddenly recalling the thrill I felt when Jamie and I had each gotten our first matching best friend tattoos. It was the week before she left for college. We wanted to remind ourselves, that no matter where life would take us, we would always be there for each other.

"Hey... You wanna get a tattoo after brunch?" I suggested, pointing at the shop across the street.

"That sounds like fun." She replied. "What do you wanna get?"

"I don't know, maybe a butterfly or something small. We can look up some art for inspiration while we're waiting for our table."

"Yeah, OK! Let's do it!" Jamie agreed, enthusiastically.

Jamie and I shared the Plaza Cafe's famous Croissant French Toast and an order of their corned beef hash as we pondered over tons of tattoo art.

I loved how Jamie was always so willing to go along with my crazy plans. After combing through tons of tattoo art, Jamie settled on a constellation piece of the stars when she was born. I chose a piece that portrayed the transformation of a caterpillar to a butterfly.

The sting of the needle was oddly a welcoming experience. I just wanted to feel... something. Jamie's was finished before I was ready, so she came over to where I was sitting in the chair with my arm stretched out.

"What do you think? Do you like it?" She asked, turning around as she lifted her hair to show me her new tattoo on the back of her neck.

"It looks great!" I said. I was trying not to flinch and mess up the artist's handy work.

"Oh my god, yours looks so good! I love the colors!" Jamie cried, when the artist wiped away the ink from my wrist with a tissue. "I'm gonna go get us some tattoo balm. We can share it, so don't worry about getting your own."

The artist was wrapping up my tattoo, when Jamie returned. She was holding a small black bag in her hand. "I got a new tongue ring too. They have some really cute stuff, here!" I was happy to see Jamie enjoying our little adventure.

~

When we arrived back home, I was feeling tired and ready for a nap. As we approached the door to the lobby, I stopped in my tracks and pulled Jamie with me behind the corner, before she could open the door.

"Wait! Don't go in there…. That's Lena! Why is she here?" When we peeked our heads around the corner, Lena appeared to be arguing with the security guard.

"That *is* her!" Jamie shouted in a whisper. "Maybe I should go in there and see what they're arguing about. I can listen in while I get the mail. She doesn't know who I am."

"You're right. She doesn't. I'll walk around to the main entrance. Text me when the coast is clear!" I said, as I headed for the outside exit of the parking garage. I didn't want Lena to see me, in case she left before I could disappear. I waited around the corner until I received the text from Jamie.

Jamie:

OK, she's gone! She went out through the main entrance, so be careful!

Me:

OK, thanks! She must have walked here, then. I'm coming back through the garage entrance. I'll meet you upstairs in a few!

Charlie gave me a wave as I walked through the door. He was on the phone talking with someone, so I didn't bother to stop by the desk to say hello. Instead I waved back and made my way over to the elevator.

I could tell that Jamie had some insight by the expression on her face when I walked through the door.

"Sullivan…. That's Jasper's last name, right?" She asked.

"Yes!" I replied. "Why? What did you hear?"

"I heard Charlie tell Lena that 'Mr. Sullivan' had left specific instruc-
tions not to give his new pin code out to anyone. Lena demanded that
he call him to let her upstairs and threatened to have him fired if he
didn't. I felt so bad for Charlie. I wanted to intervene, but I didn't
want to bring attention to myself."

"Oh, wow… So she was trying to get back into his penthouse. Jasper
told me in his letter that she'd been there while he was away at the lake
house. She's insane!" I said.

"Sure sounds like it!" Jamie agreed. "What a creep?!"

"Tell me about it. This is why I know I need to just stay out of this
whole mess. I never told you about the night we went to dinner for
Sam's birthday, did I?" I asked.

"No, you didn't." Jamie replied with a laugh. "but I bet you will now."

I went on to tell Jamie all the details about Sam's birthday dinner and
the tension I felt from the energy pouring out from everyone at the
table.

"Can you believe she had the audacity to sit there, drinking wine in
Jasper's face, knowing fully well that she was pregnant with his child?
Apparently she told Sam, who believes this baby belongs to him, that

the doctor said it was fine to have a glass or two." I said.

"Wow. I feel bad for Jasper. I really like him. He seems like the perfect match for you, but I think you're right. You should trust your instincts about steering clear from all of this. It almost sounds like he's the one who needs a restraining order now." Jamie said.

"You're probably right about that," I laughed. "but I can understand the delicacy of the situation. She's pregnant with his only child. He told me he plans on taking care of her if he finds out that this baby truly is his. It sounds to me like he has his doubts, though."

"Yeah, I remember what he said in the letter about her wanting his money. Sounds like Jasper's in a sticky situation, all around." Jamie stated.

"Tell me about it." I agreed.

Chapter 17

Spoiler Alert! If you're curious and want more insight behind the mystery of this story, you can skip to the hidden chapter in the back of this book! Mystery Lovers, wait until the end and keep reading.

Jasper

I let Lucas out into the backyard while I set out to survey the land on my new property. The contractors were doing most of the work inside the house and I was intending to do my best at staying out of their way. Most of the work I had planned to do was outside, anyway. The plants and trees were all overgrown and needing to be trimmed. The courtyard had the perfect space for me to plant a vegetable garden. I remembered Carla telling me how much she loved to cook and thought she would appreciate the option to choose whatever she might need for her recipes, straight from the garden.

I was relying heavily on my hopes she might one day change her mind and come back to me. I would continue my plans of making this a home she would love. I couldn't bear the thought of living here without her. I bought this place for us! That was all before I knew about this baby situation with Lena. *Ahh! Who the hell am I kidding? It's all too much!* She has her whole life ahead of her. She's not ready to play step mom. She deserves to have her *own* child when she's good and ready. Now is clearly not that time for her. I have to let her go. She deserves so much more than this. She deserves better than me and what I have to offer.

That evening, when the sun began to make its way across the October sky, Lucas and I had just returned from our walk out to the lake. After hearing the last of the construction crew trucks drive off, I took Lucas inside the house to feed him. It had been a long hard day, working out in the sun, but everything was planted in the garden.

I was anxious to grab a shower and get to work on scanning through the security footage. I didn't even know what I was looking for, but I was determined to find some answers to these questions that were burning inside my mind.

After a few hours of searching, I had finally come across something that piqued my interest. There was a car parked outside the club for several hours during non business hours. If I zoomed all the way in, it was evident that someone was inside the car, but the image was too blurry for me to see what they looked like or whether they were male or female. *Damn it!* This was going to take a lot longer than I had imagined. There were so many different angles where the camera picked up on to consider. I finally gave up and went to bed. Tomorrow was another day.

Chapter 18

⁓⚬⚬⚬⁓

Friday, October 26, 2012

Carla

The sun was set high in the afternoon sky on my walk home from work at the coffee shop. The birds were rather chatty, too. Even though I was beginning to adapt to my life without Jasper, I still felt very drawn to him in spirit. I just couldn't seem to shake him off my mind, no matter how hard I tried. I could be doing the most mundane things, and out of nowhere, I would get lost in a memory we shared inside my mind. Those thoughts always led me to feel like he could turn the corner at any moment. I often wondered if he was thinking about me half as much as I was thinking about him. Regardless of these continued reminders, I still remained in my decision to keep my distance. Even though it killed me, I knew that it was all for the best.

The only physical communication we shared since he'd left for the lake house was the letter he had written me before he left and a few scattered photos of work he was doing on the lake house he would send me by text. I would only react to those messages letting him know that I had seen them, but I would never respond with words.

It was damn near eating me up, but like everything else, I kept it all inside. I didn't confide in Jamie or Brooke or anyone else about it. Instead, I would lay in bed each night and talk to Jasper in my mind. I had so many things to say to him that I knew I wouldn't be able to in reality. I dreamed about him often, and sometimes the dreams felt so real, I would wake up and have to remind myself that it was only a dream. This was beyond obsession. I was really beginning to think that I was going crazy.

When I walked in through the door of Jamie's apartment, I was surprised to see Jamie on the couch watching TV.

"You're home early, what's the occasion?" I asked, while setting my purse down on the breakfast bar.

"All classes were canceled because of the storm." She replied. "Haven't you seen the news?"

"You know I don't watch the news." I replied as I plopped myself down on the couch next to her. "It's always so depressing."

"Well, you may wanna take a look at this!" She said as she turned the volume up on the TV.

"What's wrong with the fabric softener we use now?" I teasingly asked.

93

"Nothing is wrong with our fabric softener, smart ass!" She replied with a giggle. "It's on a commercial, keep watching."

I watched the cute furry little bear disappear from the screen as the weather girl took his place. She was standing in front of a large screen that showed the projected path of Hurricane Sandy. It was currently a category 3 storm that left casualties in Jamaica and Haiti before barreling through eastern Cuba and into the Bahamas, according to the reporter.

"By Sunday evening, the mild weather we've been enjoying here in New England may be replaced with Sandy's fury. The National Weather Service is advising everyone to make preparations now as this storm is set to hit New England early next week!"

"Oh wow. A hurricane? What should we do?" I asked.

"We don't have to worry too much about that here, that's what we pay maintenance fees for. We should probably stock up on groceries and flash lights and maybe fill our gas tanks up, just in case of anything." Jamie replied. "I'll go to the grocery store tonight while you're at work."

Jamie and I both turned our heads when my phone began ringing from my purse where I'd left it on the counter. I ran over to catch it before it stopped and pulled it out of my purse just in time to see that it was Detective Stacy calling.

"Hello?" There was no answer on the other end of the call.

"Hello?" I asked again, just in case she didn't hear me. Still nothing. *Damn it!*

"Who's that?" Jamie called out from the couch.

"It's the detective who's working AJ's case, but I missed her." I replied.

"Well, call her back! She probably has news about AJ." Jamie demanded.

"I will. Hold on." I said as I began to search for her name in the directory of my phone, when the notification of her voicemail came through. "Wait. She left a voicemail."

I brought my phone with me over to the living room and listened to the voicemail on speaker phone so Jamie could hear what she said.

"Carla, this is Detective Stacy calling to let you know that AJ has been sentenced to seven years in the Virginia state prison. You will be informed on all updates with his case, but feel free to contact me if you have any further questions, you have my number."

"Holy shit!" Jamie said. "You got' em!" Jamie was clearly ecstatic to hear the news. Where I, on the other hand, felt a handful of mixed emotions. More than anything, I was relieved to know I wouldn't have to worry about him contacting my family again. *But damn.... Seven years! He'll be 33 years old before he gets out!*

"Yeah... we got him, alright." I hummed, before nervously flashing a smile in Jamie's direction. "I'm gonna grab a nap before work, I'll see you tonight when I get off."

"Okay, sleep well." Jamie said before I headed off to my bedroom.

~

Maggie looked tired when I arrived at Silver Linings.

"Can you sort these in alphabetical order for me and stack them up so we can file them later, please?" Maggie asked as she piled a 3 foot stack of files on top of my desk. "I'm pretty swamped, so hold my calls and take a message for me, will ya?"

"You got it!" I replied, cheerfully. I was more than happy to relieve her of the workload.

"Thanks, sweetheart." Maggie said before rushing off, back to her office.

A few minutes later, I heard a text notification come through on my phone. I turned it over on my desk to see who it was from. It was Jamie, sending me the image of a flier to a Halloween Costume Party at Club Hush. It was for tomorrow night at 10 pm.

Jamie:

Wanna go? Breana sent it to me and she's asking if we're coming.

Me:

I don't have a costume!

Jamie:

I'll get one for you when I go shopping for storm supplies tonight. We should go to celebrate AJ's case! Besides... we've both been working so hard lately, we deserve a night out, don't you think? You're still a size

7, right?

Me:

Yes. I doubt you'll find anything this late, all the good costumes are probably gone by now.

Jamie:

Don't you worry about that, you can leave that up to me. Are you in?

Me:

Okay, fine. Count me in!

Jamie:

Sweet, I'll tell her we're coming and have Dillon meet us there, He's staying over this weekend. FYI

I took a look at the pile of folders on my desk and began sorting them in alphabetical order for Maggie. The idea of going to Club Hush without Jasper seemed odd to me. But Jamie was right. We did deserve to let loose a little bit. I let myself get lost in the fantasy of running into him. For all I knew, he just might be there. It was *his* club, after all. I knew I was wrong to let myself long for him, but knowing I couldn't have him made the temptation of potentially seeing him all that much sweeter.

No sooner than I had let myself slip into a reminiscent daydream about the last night we did spend together, did he walk right through the front door, carrying the end of a ladder. Andrew, the gardener he brought in to replace him followed behind holding the other end. *What the fuck?!* My jaw dropped.

"Jasper!" I let his name escape my lips in surprise. *What's he doing here?* I thought he was at his lake house.

Jasper tipped his hat to me in acknowledgment. "Angel, I mean… Carla." He said, trying to hold back his smile, but I could clearly see that lone dimple peeking out at me. With the ladder in his hands, he had no choice but to keep on going. With his back to me, I was able to get a good look at him from behind. It was obvious that whatever he was working on had him sweating through his white t-shirt. The light wash jeans he wore instantly gave way to my sudden lust. "We can bring it to the other side. I'll just be a minute." I heard him say to Andrew when they passed by my desk. I gulped.

I straightened myself up with a huff of a breath, and hoped to God that I didn't look like a hot mess. Wherever he was going, he was sure to be back very soon by what I heard him say to Andrew. My nerves were crawling at me to look my best at not assuming his reappearance, so I dove into the pile of folders on my desk.

Almost an entire month had passed since we'd parted ways from each other and just like that, the magic in the air reappeared in full force. The butterflies inside my core rose to the occasion to a point where it was impossible to deny the energy I felt flowing through my veins. It was crazy, how alive I felt, knowing he might be turning the corner at any minute. With my energy on high alert, I made my way through half the stack in front of me before Jasper made his way back to my desk. My heart was beating a mile a minute. *Why was I so freaking nervous?*

"Hey…. I was gonna text you to let you know I might be here, but I honestly thought I would be finished by now." Jasper said as he perched his rear on the far corner of my desk. He wiped the sweat pouring off his brow, before turning the ball cap he was wearing backwards on his head.

"Oh?" Was the only word my lips could form, as I dared myself to look up from the stack of folders in front of me into his flaming blue sapphire eyes. A direct connection to the flush of heat beginning to form inside my cheeks, as I suddenly felt hot.

"What are you working on?" I asked, trying hard not to reveal the fact that my insides were burning hot with desire. *He's off limits!* I told myself in silence.

"I got here at the crack of dawn, hoping we could wrap things up before you got here, but these old shutters have been giving us hell. I didn't want you to feel uncomfortable with me being here." Jasper said, as he took a swig from the bottle of water he had in his hands. *Uncomfortable? That was an understatement!*

"It's not a bother…." I huffed out. "I mean," I cleared my throat. "you're not bothering me." *Awkward!*

"Are you okay? You look a little flush, Angel?" *Angel! What was he trying to do to me?* "I mean… Carla. Jesus! I'm sorry." Jasper began to tug on his newly grown goatee. A look I was more than willing to get used to. *What am I saying? Stop it, Carla! You can't have him… He's having a baby with LENA!!!* The tension between us was more than

99

palpable, and we both knew it. I was damn near begging my body to behave. God only knew what was going on in his mind.

"So you're putting up shutters?" I asked, fighting the urge to bat my eyelashes.

"Yeah, we have a hurricane coming. I had to come help Andrew board up. You know I grew up here, I would hate to see anything happen to this place." The smell of his sweat only made things worse. *Why was I so damn attracted to him?* I wondered as I shifted my legs underneath the desk where at least he couldn't see. I swear, I'd never been this way with any man before he came into the picture.

"That makes sense." I said, nervously.

"Well, it sure looks like you've got your work cut out for you, and I still have a few hours left before we finish, so maybe we should both get back to work." He said as he stood up from my desk. "It's nice to see you." He said, with a flash of his sexy smile. I almost died.

"Yes. Same. I mean, it was good seeing you too." I could barely catch my breath. *Just go, please before I embarrass myself even more!*

Once he was gone, I finished off the pile of folders on my desk and set it in a neat stack for Maggie. The phone lines were eerily quiet for the rest of the day, which was good for Maggie. Jasper steered clear from my view, thankfully. I saw his SUV parked outside when I was leaving, but I was pretty sure he was still working on the other side of the property. It felt strange for me to leave and not say goodbye to him, but deep down, I knew it was for the best.

My phone rang when I got in my car. It was Mama.

"Hi Mama. How are you?" I asked, as I answered her call.

"I'm good, baby. How are you?" She asked.

"I'm good." I replied. "I'm just leaving the office to head home."

"I was just watching the news and saw there's a big hurricane coming your way. Hurricane Sandy. Are you girls gonna be alright?" She asked.

"Oh. Yes. I saw it too! Jamie's out getting us some hurricane supplies. How's Abby?" I asked.

"Abby's good. She should be home soon. She's out with her friends."

"OK, well, please tell her I said hi!" I said.

"I will. You'll keep me informed about the storm?" She asked.

"Yes. We should be fine. I'll be sure to call you once the storm passes." I said.

"OK, you know I still worry about you." She said, clearly concerned.

"I know. I'll be in touch! I Promise." I reassured her.

"I love you, baby. Talk to you soon." She said.

"Love you too, Mama. Bye." I said before ending the call. I turned on the ignition and headed home, excited to see what Jamie was able to come up with for our costumes.

Chapter 19

"You have got to be kidding me!" I said to Jamie when she showed me my costume.

"What? You don't like it?" She asked, with a devilish grin.

"Well, no. It's not that! It's beautiful." I said, as I held the slinky looking white dress against my body while staring at my reflection in her full length mirror. Apparently, I would be walking into Club Hush tomorrow evening dressed as an angel with giant wings and a sparkle halo that would cling into my hair with clips.

"I thought it was perfect! All they had left were accessories at the costume store. I sent a pic to Breana and she made me come over to pick out some dresses from her closet to go with them. Here's mine." Jamie said as she stepped out of her closet holding up a black leotard with a red tutu skirt attached in one hand, and the bag containing the accessories of her costume in her other. "Do you think Dillon will like it?"

"Omg! That's adorable! How could he not?" I replied, as I imagined Jamie dressed in her Devil costume.

~

Later that night as I lay in bed, I found myself fantasizing about Jasper before I went to sleep, again. That little magic bubble was back! I could feel it crawling beneath every pore of my skin. No matter how hard I tried to fight it, I just couldn't seem to hold back my feelings for him. They were just so raw and unlike anything I had ever experienced with anyone else. It made me wonder what our lives would be like if our situation were different. If only he had never got that stupid phone call! *Would we still be together?* I let my thoughts begin to wonder as I recaptured our run in earlier that afternoon.

The moment we entered each other's presence, I could feel the intertwining of our energy. It was like we were both dancing to the beat of our desire for one another. The element of forbidden fruit only seemed to make me want him more. The magnetism between us was so strong, it lingered on as we parted. But just like any drug, you can never have too much of a good thing before you get burned. Allowing myself to slip into this fantasy felt dangerous, but in such a good way. I honestly don't know if I was strong enough to fight this current, but I knew I had to.

~

Jasper

It felt good to be back home. I came back a few times to grab some things and check on my apartment. This time, I would finally get to sleep in my own bed and not that God awful air mattress. Even Lucas seemed happy to be home, as I watched him snooze away in his own bed inside his crate.

Most of the work on the lake house property was finished. I already had hurricane force windows installed, but figured it best to add some storm shutters for added security, just in case. Thankfully this was all done before I even knew about this storm coming, so all I had to do now was buy some furniture and decorate. I could have done that a week ago, but I had been procrastinating. My heart just wasn't in it. Carla was supposed to be a big part of this plan. When I bought this property, I imagined her helping me decorate everything to her liking. It was supposed to be the fun part, but without her insight as I initially planned, the task felt more daunting than anything else.

Seeing her today at the office was like a breath of fresh air to my depleted lungs. I wanted to take her in my arms and kiss her so badly, but I knew that wasn't what she wanted or needed. I thought maybe after some distance apart, my feelings for her may have let up a little, but they were stronger than ever, instead. The way she reacted to my being there told me that she felt it too. She was fighting it with everything she had, just like I was.

I hated being in this position. I hadn't talked to Sam or Lena in over a month now. I wondered what was going on with them. The way Lena had been neglecting herself and this baby with her drinking made me wonder how healthy this baby could even be. It made me sick to my stomach knowing that my child could be depending on her for its needs and there wasn't a single thing I could do about it.

Half of me wanted to apply a forceful hand at getting her to stop drinking, but that was damn near impossible without Sam knowing that this baby could be mine. I should have come out and told him, but I didn't want to break his heart. One thing I knew for certain was that Sam loved Lena with everything he had, no matter how much I couldn't stand her, myself.

The other half of me seemed to be the one I let take over. I was pretending this baby wasn't even mine in the first place. Until I had solid evidence that it truly was, a part of me would never believe it.

Just like every night I had spent at the lake house, I opened up my laptop to do my late night detective work. After seeing that car parked outside the club on numerous occasions, I knew that something was up. I just didn't know what it was. *Who the hell was watching us?* I wondered as I began scrolling through the footage looking for something that might catch my eye.

When I found a clip of Eddie walking into the club during daylight hours, I knew something was fishy. *What the hell was he doing there?* I wrote down the date and time on the footage so I could cross check the images from a camera view inside the club. It was then that I found some sort of exchange happen between him and Sam. I had to zoom in on the image. Sam was handing him cash for what looked like a bottle of pills. *Are you fucking kidding me?* This didn't make any sense! Sam hadn't shown me any signs of using drugs. If he was using, he knew how to hide it well, that was for damn sure! I clicked over to another screen, determined to find out more, when all of a sudden, my screen went dead. *Shit! I forgot to charge my laptop.*

It had been a long day of work, getting those shutters up in the hot sun. I was tired. Too tired to wait until my laptop charged. I hit the showers and went to bed. Detective Jasper's work would have to wait another day, until tomorrow.

As I lay in bed, I caught myself wondering if Carla was thinking about me as much as I was thinking about her. I couldn't stop replaying our moment together in the office, in my mind. She was so nervous. It only fueled the fire inside my heart for her even more. She looked good, though, could I really blame myself?

Chapter 20

The next morning, Lucas and I went for our run in the park like always. Afterwards, I went to the Silver Linings property to finish up a few things for Maggie in preparation for the storm. I made a supply run and dropped everything off before heading back home.

I thought about stopping by the club to check up on how things were going. Even though I owned half of the club, the whole idea was Sam's to begin with. He said he only needed me to supply the money to help him get it started and that he was fully capable of managing it all on his own. Based on the reports we both had access to and the continuous deposits into my bank account, everything seemed to be lining up just fine without me being there. I trusted Sam. He was my best friend. He never gave me any reason to doubt him in that sense.

Thanks to Tony and the access code he gave me, I could easily keep a watch on things from a distance. Rather than have a run in I wasn't prepared to have with Sam and Lena, I opted to pick up some Chinese takeout for dinner, instead.

After taking Lucas out for his walk, I came home to settle in and review some more security footage from the club. This was becoming an obsession. I was beginning to feel like a real life, detective.

It was almost midnight when I shockingly received a phone call from Carla's number. It was pretty late for her to be calling me. Normally, she would be in bed by now.

"Hello?" I said, quickly answering her call. Loud music poured in from the background.

"Heyyy, Stranger…. You answered." She giggled. Her voice sounded strange. It was long and drawn out and her pitch was higher than normal. *Was that a hiccup? Is she drunk?*

"Carla?" I asked to confirm it was really her.

"Peek a boo!" She laughed. "Are you surprised?" Another hiccup. "It's me?" She laughed.

"Where are you? Have you been drinking?" I asked, growing concerned.

"I'm here…" She hummed. " But you're not. Everyone is here, but you're not. Why aren't you here, Jasper?" She asked. "You should be here."

Judging by the sound of the music in the background and her assumption that I *should* be there, I figured she was at Club Hush.

"I'm not there. I'm home... With Lucas." I said, quickly scanning the current security footage to find out where she was. It only took a minute to find her sitting on one of the lounge sofas. "Where's Jamie? Is she there with you?" I asked.

"Dancing. They're all dancing. It's a party!" Carla replied.

The club was only about a 15 minute drive away, I could easily be there in 10. I just needed her to stay in place. The last thing she needed was to be left alone and vulnerable for the taking of some asshole.

"Stay where you are, I'm coming!" I said, as I swiftly rose to my feet and grabbed my keys from off the table. I tried to keep her on the line, but the call dropped when I got inside the elevator.

~

When I arrived at the club, I pulled into the valet and told them to keep my car running. Perks of being the owner, I suppose. I didn't know how I was going to do it, but my intention was to go in and grab her before anyone noticed my being there. I kept my hoody on, hoping I would go unnoticed. I was surprised to see everyone dressed in costume. I had been so busy working at the lake house, I had forgotten it was almost Halloween.

The last thing I had expected was to see *my angel* sprawled out on the couch, sitting next to that asshole Eddie! *FUCK!* His hands were on her thigh, and he was trying to get her to kiss him, but she was clearly passed out.

"What the fuck are you doing?" I asked, breaking the two of them up.""She's passed out, you sick fuck!" I said, with a swift punch to Eddie's jaw. He was too busy with his hands all over Carla to see it coming. It damn near knocked him senseless. I wasn't here to fight, though. I didn't want to bring any more attention to myself than necessary.

"Carla! Baby, wake up!" When she didn't respond, I picked her up and carried her over my shoulder, as I darted for the exit. I didn't make my way out without catching Sam's attention from across the bar. He tried to call me over, but I ignored him and kept going. I knew if I had paid him no mind, I could escape before he was able make it through the crowd to get to me.

"Open the passenger door, please and help me buckle her in. Hurry!" I said to the valet guy. He knew I meant business by my tone, and was quick to jump to the task. I got into the driver's side and slipped him a $100 bill and pulled out of the parking lot as fast as I could.

When I pulled into the parking garage of my apartment building, I figured it best to leave Carla where she lay since she barely stirred at all, the entire ride home. I adjusted the seat back for her so she would be a little more comfortable before heading upstairs. I walked into the lobby and found Freddy behind the security desk.

"Hi Freddy. Do me a favor please... Keep a watch on my car in the garage, will ya? I'll be down in a few minutes."

"Sure thing, Mr. Sullivan." The staff were always more than willing to adhere to my requests because they all knew I took good care of them. I took the elevator and hurried upstairs to go pack a bag and grab Lucas. I brought extra t shirts and sweats for Carla, because I knew she would need something to change into at some point. I didn't have any of her clothes inside my penthouse. I also grabbed my laptop because it was clear, I needed it to keep a better watch on the club.

I knew that Sam saw me, but I wasn't sure if Lena had. Either way, I wasn't taking any chances on sticking around to see if either one of them showed up here to come find me. I put Lucas's collar and leash on and grabbed my bag and headed back down to the lobby.

"Thanks buddy. This is for you." I said as I handed Freddy some cash, while trying to keep Lucas from running out the door. "If anyone calls or comes by, just tell them I'm out of town. Do not let anyone upstairs."

"Yes, sir."

"Can you hold my bag and keep watching while I run him outside real quick? I'll be back in a minute." It was a long ride out to the lake house, I didn't want to take any chances. I knew he had to go.

"You got it, sir! Thank you!" Freddy said with a flash of his pearly white dentures.

Thankfully, Lucas was quick with his business. I came back to the lobby to grab my bag, and took Lucas to the car. Carla was still sleeping. After loading Lucas into the back seat, I pulled a sweater out of my bag to use as a blanket for Carla. She barely moved an inch from when I'd left her. I sat for a minute, watching her breathe to make sure she was OK and took off for the lake house. I had no idea how much she'd had to drink. It couldn't have been *that* much, the club was barely open 2 hours when she called me.

When I pulled into the driveway, Carla was still sleeping. I let Lucas inside and came back for her. I tried to wake her, but she was out cold. It was a bit of a challenge to get her out of my car, but I eventually did. I carried her inside the house and laid her out onto the air mattress in the bedroom. I was really kicking myself for not buying the bed I should have bought a week ago. The previous owners left their living room furniture, and although it was plain to see why they were leaving it, I was thankful that I hadn't gotten rid of it yet. At least we would have somewhere to sit until the storm passed.

It wasn't the most ideal situation, but I knew that we were safe here, away from all the drama in my life. The lake was far enough from the house and with the impact windows and newly installed hurricane shutters, I felt it was as secure as could be if we needed to ride the storm out here.

I dragged the ratty old arm chair from the living room and brought it into the bedroom. I just sat there, watching her sleep. She looked like a real life angel. I wondered what made her think to wear this costume. From the way she spoke on the phone with me, it was obvious, she thought I would be there. *Was she trying to get my attention?* I wondered.

I wanted so badly to climb into the bed and just lay there next to her, but out of respect for her wishes, I refused to let myself give into that temptation. Instead, I fell asleep in the chair. I wanted to be there in case she woke up in the middle of the night wondering where she was, but that never happened.

It was almost 8 am when I woke up the next morning with a terrible crick in my neck. Carla was still sleeping and Lucas was nudging at my fingers.

"Alright boy, let's go." I whispered as I grabbed a hold of Lucas by his collar and quietly slipped out of the room to take him outside.

Chapter 21

Carla

An assault to my senses awoke me to the smell of fresh paint that was so strong, I felt sick to my stomach. I opened my eyes and took a moment to gather my surroundings. The light of day peeking in through the window didn't reveal very much. The room was cold and empty, except for an old dusty looking armchair next to the bed I was lying in. *Where am I?* I wondered, as confusion set in. I swung my feet down to the floor to brace myself to stand up. *Why am I sleeping on an air mattress? And why do I feel so weak?* I took a hard swallow. My mouth felt very dry, like I was extremely dehydrated. I had trouble getting myself to stand up from the bed from where it lay on the floor.

As panic began to settle in, my need to vomit quickly took over. I needed to find somewhere to puke. That smell was only making things worse. I had never been so affected by the smell of paint before, but my head felt like it was going to explode.

I reached for the handle on the door and found my way out of the room I was in, to find a long, dark hallway. I had no idea where I was and my balance was off as I stumbled down the hallway, determined to find a bathroom. I was hoping that once I got whatever was trying to leave my system out, I might feel a little better.

As I opened each door each door I came across, I only found empty bedrooms filled with more of that God awful paint smell. Finally, after my third door, I found a room with a toilet. And it was right on time. No sooner than I lifted the toilet seat, did everything come hurling out of me like that scene from the Exorcist.

After several minutes of continuous vomiting, the rest became dry heaves. I let myself sink against the cold tile of the bathroom floor to let my body settle from all the puking. When I finally felt safe enough to stand up, I had to grab hold of the sink to help me keep my balance. I turned on the faucet and splashed some cold water over my face and looked into the mirror. I was a mess. I had makeup smeared all over my face. I was dressed like an angel, but I looked like death! I shook my head, but it only reminded me of my pounding headache. *Why am I wearing an Angel costume?* I desperately tried to recall the details of the previous night, so I could remember how I got here. As I slowly began to get my bearings, I stared at my reflection. It was only a moment later that I was startled by the shadow of a figure coming up behind me in the doorway. *Jasper?* I turned around to face him. I was embarrassed for him to see me in the condition I was in, but more relieved than ever that he was here.

"You're awake." He said, cautiously.

"Where am I, Jasper? I can't remember anything. Why can't I

remember?" I asked.

"You look pale, why don't we get you settled somewhere so you can lie down and I'll explain everything I know." He replied, warmly.

"Okay," I agreed.

After watching me struggle with my balance, Jasper swept me up off my feet and carried me out of the bathroom, down the hallway to where the house opened up into a wider and brighter space. I was grateful that my sudden wave of nausea seemed to be gone. The smell of bacon and coffee seemed far more welcoming than the smell of paint. He settled me down on an old brown sofa, where I could lie down. The furniture seemed so odd and out of place in the sleekness of the space that we were in, but I was far from complaining.

"I thought you might be hungry, so I made us some breakfast. Wait here."

A few minutes later, Jasper returned with a paper plate of eggs and bacon and a paper cup filled with orange juice. He set it down on the old wooden coffee table that sat in front of the sofa he had me laid upon.

"There's coffee too, but I figured you might need to eat something first." He said.

"I can use some water, if that's alright?" I asked.

"Of course. I'll be right back." He said.

He soon returned with a cold bottle of Fiji water from the fridge. He opened the cap and handed it to me to drink. I sat up on the couch and drank nearly half the bottle before I finally stopped for air. I could swear that bottle had magic inside it, as it seemed to bring me back to life. Well, at least for the most part. I still felt awful, but the cold water made me feel so much better.

"Thank you," I said, extremely grateful. My mouth felt like the Mojave Desert. Jasper proceeded to tell me everything he remembered from the night before. I couldn't believe the situation with Eddie. It was a good thing Jasper came and found me when he did, or God only knew where I would've ended up. The last thing I could recall was getting ready with Jamie in our apartment before we left for the costume party at Club Hush.

"Here, have something to eat, I'm sure it will give you some strength and help you feel better, if you can manage to hold it down." Jasper said, handing me my plate from off the coffee table.

I took a few bites. "Mmm, thank you." I said, trying to keep my mouth closed so he wouldn't see me chewing. "So where exactly are we?" I asked.

Jasper took a deep breath and crouched down beside me. "We're at at the lake house." *Was he nervous?* "I know it needs some love... and furniture," he laughed, "but I haven't really gotten that far yet. All of the renovations are finished, though."

"It's really nice." I said as I watched him walk over to the kitchen to grab some orange juice out of the fridge. My stomach began to flip flop nervously like it normally would when he was present. Delayed response. Maybe the food really *was* making me feel better. I laughed silently at my thoughts. My head was still pounding though.

Jasper set his breakfast plate and our glasses of orange juice down on the coffee table and pulled up a folding chair to sit down beside me and eat.

"How are you feeling?" He asked. He swiped a slice of bacon from his plate before popping into his mouth.

"A lot better. But my head hurts." I replied.

"I'm afraid I don't have any Tylenol here. Maybe we should venture out for some supplies after we finish breakfast."

"Supplies?" I asked, sounding confused.

"You know we have that storm coming, right?" He asked.

"You're right, I forgot." I said. I was still a little groggy. I barely remembered the situation we were in, because it felt so natural being with him, aside from the pent up sexual tension lurking between us.

"When is it supposed to come?" I asked.

"Tomorrow." He replied, with a chuckle. "You really are a bit disoriented, aren't you?" I was starting to feel my face flush from embarrassment. "Don't worry, Angel…. I mean… Carla." He bit his lip and cleared his throat. I suddenly felt the heat transfer from my face down to the core of my belly. "We're safe here. I had impact windows installed, and we also have the hurricane shutters."

"Well that sounds comforting to know." I said, trying to mask the rush of nerves going off inside my belly.

Chapter 22

After breakfast, Jasper gave me a tour around the property and showed me his plans for the garden he planted. The 2.5 acre property was beautiful and had a privacy fence that would keep Lucas from running free. Jasper showed me all of the trees had planted to bring a more charming curb appeal.

After the tour, we let Lucas back inside the house. I took a shower in the state of the art bathroom Jasper had installed inside his master suite and got dressed in a pair of Jasper's sweats and a t-shirt he had brought for me. When we were ready, we set out for our trip to the store for supplies.

I found my purse on the floorboard of Jasper's SUV. It was then that I discovered my phone and the slew of missed text messages and calls from Jamie. I didn't even bother to read the texts or listen to my voicemail. I quickly dialed her number to call and let her know where I was. The phone rang once and she answered immediately.

"Carla! Thank God! Where have you been?" She asked.

"I'm with Jasper." I replied, I couldn't match her energy, even if I tried. "We're at his lake house. Well, technically we're out getting supplies for this storm."

"I didn't even know that Jasper was there, but forget all that! Did you guys see what happened? What time did you guys leave?"

"No. I can't seem to remember anything from last night," I replied. "Jasper told me everything he knew. He came to pick me up after I drunk dialed him."

"Well, first off, Eddie got punched in the face. Then someone got shot! Carla, they said it was the owner of the club! If Jasper's with you, then it must have been his friend, Sam!"

"Hold on. Slow down, Jamie. I'm putting you on speaker phone." I said as I clicked over to the speaker button on my phone. "Say that again, please!"

"I think it was Sam who got shot!" Jamie repeated herself. "It was total chaos! We all ran when we heard the gunshots."

Jasper quickly took the phone from my hands and started talking to Jamie. "Are you sure? Do you know if he's okay?"

"All I know is that he was rushed to the hospital. Dillon and I were gone by the time the ambulance showed up. Alex and Mandy saw everything." Jasper pulled over on the side of the road and handed me back my phone. He found the number for the hospital on his own cell and quickly dialed it to see if he could get an update on Sam.

"I was so worried about you, we couldn't find you anywhere!" Jamie continued.

"I'm okay. I'm sorry I didn't call you. I don't know how I got so drunk. I can't seem to remember a thing from last night. Apparently, I slept through the entire trip here and didn't wake up until this morning." I said.

"I'm just glad you're OK, thank God! Sounds like Jasper got you out of there in time, before everything went down. I was terrified!"

"I'm so glad you guys are okay. I didn't mean to make you worry." I said.

"So are you staying there for the storm?" Jamie asked.

"I don't know. I'll keep you posted. I should probably let you go. Jasper's on the phone with the hospital, trying to find out what's up with Sam."

"Okay. Keep me posted!" Jamie said before she ended the call. Jasper was still on the phone when I hung up with Jamie.

"I'm still on hold. I know he's alive, but that's all I know." Jasper said.

"OK, thank you. What room is he in?" I heard him ask the person on the other end of the line. "Thanks." Jasper said before ending his call with the hospital.

"He can't have any visitors right now. They told me to wait until after the storm." Jasper said to me.

"I'm so sorry, Jasper. I know he's your best friend," I said, trying to console him. I rested my hand on top of his, across his lap. Jasper's Adam's apple rose in his throat. I could feel every bit of emotion running through him when we touched. He was trying to hide it, but I could feel it all.

"He's like my brother." He choked out and shook his head. "He's gonna pull through. I know he will. I just hate the way things are between us right now."

"I can imagine." I said, as Jasper turned on the ignition and turned back onto the road. We drove in silence the whole way to the store. I found it odd that there were barely any clouds in the sky and the trees were all still as can be. By the looks of things, it was difficult to tell that we even had a storm coming our way.

Chapter 23

⁣

When we got to the store, the place was a madhouse. Many people were lined up to pick up their last minute supplies for the storm. Our first stop was the medicine aisle to get some Advil so I could get rid of my lingering headache. Jasper handed me a bottle of water from the only 2 cases we could find that were left on the shelves. I couldn't get that bottle of Advil open any faster than I did.

"I guess we should grab a can opener and some candles, in case we lose power." Jasper said to me, as an elderly lady nearly crashed into our cart. Navigating through the store had proven quite a challenge with so many people in it.

"I'm so sorry. Could you reach that for me?" She asked, frantically pointing at the last loaf of bread on the shelf behind me. Jasper reached over my shoulder to hand it to her.

"Here you go." He said, as he handed her the loaf of bread. She placed it into her cart that was filled with more cans of cat food than I had ever seen anyone purchase at one time.

"I have plenty of food for us at the house." Jasper said to me as he tossed a box of crackers and a jar of peanut butter into our cart. "Why don't we go over to the electronics section. I want to see if we can find a generator. We can also use some more pillows and a better situation for a bed. That air mattress is done for."

"Okay." I said, trailing along with him.

By the time we were finished, our cart was loaded with anything we could possibly need, including several books and board games and the most expensive air bed Jasper could find. This one came with an automatic pump, the kind you plug into the wall to inflate.

My headache was finally beginning to subside. Thank God! I was gonna need a lot of patience when it came to waiting in line at check out. I still couldn't believe I was riding this storm out with Jasper at his lake house. I kept having to remind myself of his baby situation with Lena. If only that night never happened. We wouldn't be forced to keep our hands off of one another. The temptation felt like walking into an ice cream parlor and getting a good whiff of the freshly made waffle cones, knowing I was diabetic and couldn't have any. It was gonna take all the strength I had to keep myself from getting too close to him these next few days.

When we got back to the lake house, we spent most of our time playing Scrabble, and reading on the couch. We stopped in between to catch the updates of the storm that was headed in our direction on the small TV Jasper bought at the store. It felt so natural, spending time with

Jasper, despite the underlying tension he was feeling about Sam.

The hospital still refused to give him any information about Sam's condition. All he knew was that he was alive and not allowed any visitors. Jasper toyed with the idea of going back to Boston to demand answers, but figured it best to stay put with the storm coming.

When it was time to go to sleep, Jasper planned on taking the couch and offered me the bed. I felt bad and told him he could sleep in the bed with me, as long as he behaved. I secretly wanted to feel his warm body beside me, but of course, I didn't tell him that. We did wind up cuddling, but that was as far as things went between us. The desire was prominent in the tension between us, but we both stood strong in our respect for one another.

The next morning, I was the first one to wake up. Lucas followed me out of the bedroom when I went into the kitchen to brew a pot of coffee. I figured I would take him out myself so Jasper could sleep in. Lucas was so excited to go out when he saw me take the leash off the kitchen counter, I could barely get him to sit still long enough for me to put it on him. After bribing him with treats, I was finally able to get him to cooperate.

I opened the door to find a relatively calm sky, considering we would soon be met with Sandy's wrath. It was still early. The sun had barely risen past the horizon. The morning dew from the grass dampened my bare feet as I ventured out onto the property with Lucas. He really did seem happy here. I was so glad there was a fence around the property when he took off, chasing after some squirrels that were teasing him. I had to let go of the leash or he would have easily thrown me head first into the ground.

"Lucas!" I shouted out after him. Lucas kept running all the way to the sideline of pine trees aligning the fence, where the squirrels had found their escape among the branches. Lucas stopped at the treeline to bark at them. When I finally caught up to him, I bent over to pick up his leash and guided him away from the poor squirrels.

I was startled by the laughter pouring out into the breeze. I looked up to find Jasper standing outside in only a pair of sweatpants, holding a steamy cup of coffee in his hands. He must have caught the entire spectacle I had made of myself and Lucas. If I weren't so turned on by the sight of him, I may have just died right then and there from sheer embarrassment. The butterflies all took a dive, the moment we locked eyes.

"I thought you were sleeping!" I called out to him. I struggled to find my balance while keeping hold of the leash at the same time. Apparently, I overestimated my ability to keep control of the nearly hundred pound pup. *Seriously, what was I thinking? This dog weighed almost as much as I did!* I tried to keep my cool and not look too embarrassed when we finally reached over to where Jasper was standing.

"Here, give me that, silly girl." Jasper teased me with his signature smirk, as he took the leash from out of my hands.

We took a walk down to the lake and Jasper showed me the lighthouse. As soon as we got there, the wind began to pick up and the waves were beginning to show signs of the incoming storm.

"Maybe we should start heading back." Jasper said to me, quickly taking my hand in his. The jolt of energy flowing through me felt way too good to let go of his hand as he led me down the path we needed to take to get back to the house. The storm clouds were beginning to roll in. This was gonna be a long night, I thought. I continued to fight the churning of the butterflies inside my tummy, while simultaneously trying to keep up with Jasper's pace. My will to resist him was weakening every time we touched.

Miraculously, we made back inside the house, just in time to hear the crackling sound of the roaring thunder echoing through the trees. Even Lucas was panting as he headed straight for his water dish. I couldn't help but giggle at the sight of the giant pup lapping up every bit of water that was available to him inside his bowl.

We spent the afternoon sitting on the couch eating peanut butter and jelly sandwiches on crackers & microwave popcorn, while watching for updates and reading the books we'd bought at the store, in between. Jasper made another phone call to the hospital and was finally able to get a room number to reach Sam. I waited anxiously to hear what the status was when Jasper was finally able to get a hold of him.

"He's gonna be okay." Jasper said to me, before ending the call with Sam. "Apparently he took a blow to the shoulder and they're taking him in for x-rays. He says he's in a lot of pain, but it sounds to me like he's pretty heavily medicated." *Thank God!* I didn't know Sam very well at all. I'd only met him once at his birthday dinner, but I knew how important he was to Jasper.

"Oh, good." I said as I released the air I didn't realize I was holding. "That's good news!" I said. I wondered if I should ask him if he'd ever told Sam about the baby situation with Lena. We hadn't discussed it, but I had a sneaky suspicion that Jasper had yet to come clean with Sam about everything.

"I still haven't told him about the situation with Lena and this baby." Jasper admitted as if he'd read my thoughts. "It's gonna crush him when he finds out. I haven't talked to either of them since that night we left them at dinner. I know I need to, but I've been trying to find out what really happened that night. None of it makes any sense to me. I just don't understand why I can't seem to remember anything about that night."

"That sounds oddly familiar to what happened to me when I woke up here." I said.

"I've been thinking about that, too. Here, take a look at this." Jasper said. He took his laptop off the coffee table and sat it across his lap so we could see and pulled up the security camera footage from the club. He showed me clips of the car parked outside the club for several hours, then switched over to a clip he had of inside the club. Sam was making some sort of exchange with a guy who looked very familiar.

"Hey! Wait a second! Is that Eddie? Go back! Can you zoom in?" I asked. Jasper zoomed in on the shot. We could clearly see Eddie handing Sam a prescription bottle.

"Here's the weird part! I never suspected Sam of using drugs. He wasn't showing any signs to me. He always despised them, because of his dad. Do you think the pills were for Lena?" Jasper asked.

"Hmm, maybe." I replied. I didn't know Lena well enough to know any better with her either. All I knew was that her energy really put me on guard.

"Okay, well don't call me crazy..." Jasper started to say before taking a moment to consider my reaction, "when you couldn't remember anything about the night I found you with Eddie, it reminded me so much of the morning I woke up in bed with Lena. I even got sick when I got home, just like you did. Naturally, I thought it was from the alcohol, but what if we were drugged?" He asked.

"That does sound like a logical explanation, but why would someone want to drug us?" I asked.

"Well, I don't know why anyone would wanna drug you, except for how I found you with Eddie putting his sleazy hands all over you while you were passed out. As bad as Lena has been after me for this check to keep her from aborting my child, I wouldn't put it past her to scheme against me. I haven't trusted her from the moment I met her. That's why it seemed so absurd to me that I could end up in bed with her in the first place." Jasper replied. "The other thing is, I would never willingly betray Sam like that. I don't know what he sees in her, but I do know that he loves her."

"Interesting point. That does make a lot of sense, only it was Sam who took the bottle from Eddie, not Lena. And why would Sam want to drug me?"

"God only knows." Jasper shook his head. "I'm just glad I came to get you before we could find out! My God, if anything were to happen to you…." His voice trailed off.

"I'm glad you came to get me, too!" I said as the lights began to flicker.

"Uh oh. I'll go get the candles." Jasper said as he took off to go grab them from off the kitchen counter.

131

"Okay, I'll come with you." I said as I jumped to my feet to go heat up our leftovers for dinner, while we still had power. Jasper and I made a great team at getting everything we needed before the lights finally went out for good. Jasper bought the only 2 flashlights the store had left, so we ate our dinner by candle light. I thoroughly enjoyed Jasper's chili. He really was a great cook!

"Mmm... How does this taste even better than yesterday?" I asked as I spooned another cozy bite into my mouth.

"Chili always tastes better the next day." Jasper agreed. "It gives the flavors time to marinate with each other." I had to wonder if that's what was going on between us too.

Being together with Jasper was beginning to feel like my birthright. The hardest part was resisting the love I felt so deeply within my soul for him. I wanted him to kiss me so badly. I was never the type of girl to make the first move, but that didn't change the burning feeling of desire I had inside me. Being stuck in close proximity with him through this storm, with all of the elements alive that were present, the first night we made love, was honestly making me forget every reason I had cast him aside. *Ugh! Lena! Baby! Why?!?!*

~

We went to bed early that night. As I got dressed in my nightgown we'd bought at the store, and brushed my teeth in the bathroom by candle light, I wondered if I could continue to resist my urges if Jasper were to try to make a move. I knew he felt just as drawn to me as I was to him, I could feel it! I looked into the mirror and told myself to be strong. *You got this!* But, I knew that I was only lying to myself. What

I needed more than anything was for Jasper to be strong enough for the both of us.

I climbed into bed with Jasper. As we both lay awake, listening to the storm and all its fury, Jasper was the first of us to speak.

"I know this isn't the most ideal situation... The two of us, sleeping on an air mattress in the middle of a hurricane, with no power, but there's something I have to let you know." He said.

"Oh yeah?" I asked. "What's that?"

"There's no one else on earth I'd rather be with right now, than with you, Angel." He said as he wrapped his strong forearms around me from behind... *No, no no no no! Don't call me Angel, you know what that does to me!* There it was! The words we both knew would ultimately bust the door wide open to relieve the awkward sexual tension that had been rising between us all day. Just like me, Jasper was losing his will to resist the current.

"Me either." I had to admit as I turned around to face him. The air of the mattress made me sink further against his body. Instantly my body rippled with tingles. *No, no! Not those eyes, too!* The intensity of the pressure building inside me went off the charts as I melted into his sapphire gaze. Jasper smoothed my hair away from my eyes, and before I knew it, his lips were pressed deep into mine. I could feel the intensity take over us both as we crashed into one another like a freight train going off the rails with no breaks. We were headed straight for the uncharted territory. A place where neither of us was able to contain the longing we had for one another, another minute.

The heat of our kiss ignited a fiery passion we had both been missing for so long. It's a wonder how Jasper was able to muster up enough strength to break away. "I'm sorry. I told you I would behave. It's just so damn hard, when all I can think about right now is how irresistible you are." He breathed, before stealing another kiss. "Yep! You know what? I think I will take the couch!" He laughed. "Fuck! This is so much harder than I thought." Jasper laughed.

I couldn't help but laugh too. "Yeah, I think it might be a good idea to separate, but let . me take the couch instead." I offered.

"None of these options are all that great, but I want you to be more comfortable. Any chance you might be up for a midnight game of Scrabble?" He asked. "I doubt I'll be able to fall asleep right now."

"Sure, why not? I probably won't sleep either." I said.

As it turned out, Jasper was the Scrabble King. He kicked my butt, finishing the game with 87 points more than me. We took a break for some milk and Oreo cookies from our Hurricane snack stash. I challenged him to a game of Boggle. It was my favorite game and I'd never found an opponent to beat me. After 3 rounds of playing, he finally conceded the crown to me. We both finally grew tired enough to get some sleep, so we went to bed for the night. After Jasper tucked me into the couch, Lucas jumped up to snuggle in with me.

"Well at least you have some company." Jasper said, smiling before disappearing down the hall.

Chapter 24

The next morning, we took Lucas out together and surveyed the property for any signs of significant damage the storm may have caused. There were leaves covering the entire yard and some broken branches that had fallen from the trees, but overall, the property seemed to be in good shape.

"Hey, look! The garden survived!" Jasper said, proudly, as he bent over to sweep away the debris from the trees.

"Yes, it sure looks that way to me." I said, smiling at how Jasper's face lit up like a child when he discovered everything remained intact underneath the blanket of autumn colored leaves.

"Maybe we should head back to Boston." Jasper said, as he arose from where he was crouched down. "I need to get over to the hospital to see how Sam is doing and check on Aunt Maggie and everyone at Silver Linings." Jasper pulled Lucas away from tearing the garden any more than it already had been from the storm.

"Good idea! I need to call Jamie too." I agreed.

We went back in the house and got ready to leave. Jasper loaded Lucas into the car and we were soon off to head back to Boston. Some of the city streets on the way to the highway were flooded but we seemed to make it through without any problems. I called Jamie on the way back to let her know I was coming home and to see how everything fared at the apartment.

"Hey Jamie, it's Carla. Is everything okay? " I asked, when she answered the call.

"Everything is fine. We lost power last night. The power company says it should be on soon." Jamie replied.

"Really? That sucks!" I said.

"Dillon's here with me. Apparently the storm was pretty bad where he lives. His brother called to check on him and told him that traffic is a nightmare, so he's staying over again tonight." Jamie said.

"Oh, good. I felt so bad I couldn't be there with you for the storm. I'm so glad you're not alone." I said. "We lost power over here too. We're on our way back to Boston now."

"Okay. I'll make sure everyone is dressed this time." Jamie giggled.

"Great idea!" I laughed.

"OK, sounds good. We might head out in a bit to see if anything is open for breakfast, since we can't really cook anything here." She said.

"OK, well I guess I'll see you guys soon then." I said.

"See you soon, bye!" Jamie said before she ended the call.

"Jamie said they lost power too! They're expecting it to be back on soon." I said to Jasper who's attention was fixed on the road ahead of us. Traffic was beginning to slow down on the highway.

"Well, I hope so. I'll probably be gone for a little while. I'm pretty sure Aunt Maggie is gonna have plenty of work for me to do at Silver Linings. It'll be nice to come home and get a hot shower afterwards." He said, in a hopeful tone.

~

When we got to the apartment, we had to climb the stairs in order to get up to my apartment. There was a generator running the emergency light between each flight, but it was still quite dark inside the stairwell. The air was stagnant and musty, and I was out of breath by the time we reached the floor to Jamie's apartment. I felt horrible that Jasper and Lucas still had 8 more flights to go before they would reach his penthouse.

"Why don't you come inside for a bit?" I asked.

"Sure. As long as Lucas behaves." Jasper agreed, as we approached the door to Jamie's apartment. I unlocked the door with my key and we all went inside.

"Jamie? I'm here with Jasper and Lucas." I called out, wondering where she an Dillon were.

"We're out here." I heard her call out from the balcony.

I set my bag down on the kitchen pass through and Jasper looped Lucas's leash through one of the chairs in the dining room, so he wouldn't roam too far inside the apartment. "Sit down, boy." He said. Lucas complied with his request. "Attn boy! You're learning." He said with a pat to his head as Lucas laid down on the floor next to the dining room table.

I went into the kitchen to grab a bowl of water for Lucas and set it down in front of him. He was panting from the climb we made and was more than eager to drink the water I set out for him.

"Maybe we shouldn't give him too much." Jasper chuckled.

"Oh, you're probably right." I laughed as I bent down to scoop up the bowl. We stood there and watched Lucas settle himself down across the dining room floor. Jasper followed me out onto the patio where Jamie and Dillon were finishing up their breakfast.

"Hey." I said to Jamie.

"Hey, you two!" Jamie chimed back with a smile.

"Any word on how long it'll be until we get the power back on?" I asked.

"I don't know. We can't even get through on the line, anymore. All we know is that they're working on having it restored soon, according to the recording." She replied. "I'm just glad it's at least nice out here. It's way too stuffy inside without air conditioning. Here, come sit down

138

with us.." Jamie moved over to sit with Dillon, while Dillon reached out to shake Jasper's hand.

"How's it going, man?" He asked.

"Not bad. I can't stay for very long." Jasper replied, before taking a seat next to me on the other chaise lounge. "I'm sure Maggie has all sorts of things planned for me and I still have to get over to the hospital to see Sam."

"I invited them in. That climb upstairs was brutal." I said.

"Tell me about it," she said. "We had to make it too, after walking 6 blocks to find a place to get some breakfast. Everything is still closed."

The four of us exchanged tales about how we weathered the storm and caught up on all the details Jamie and Dillon could remember from the night at Club Hush. We all turned our heads to the door when we heard Lucas whimpering from inside the apartment.

"Well, I guess that's my cue." Jasper said as he stood up from chair we were sharing. "It was nice seeing you guys again. I'm glad you're both okay."

"You too, Jasper. You're welcome anytime." Jamie said.

"Wait… I'll walk you out," I said before standing to follow Jasper inside to the dining room. Jasper released Lucas from the chair he was tied to and we all headed for the front door.

"Thank you, for getting me home safe."I don't know what I would have done without you coming to my rescue.... again." I smiled before making the epic mistake of peering deep into the pool of his gorgeous blue eyes.

"Yeah, I seem to be making quite the habit of it, huh?" He said with a flash of his dimple. He reached for the knob on the door, but didn't miss the opportunity to lock eyes with my gaze. A flash of heat raced through my body, as our energy became magnetic. My will was weak.

"Well, I guess I better go." He said as he and Lucas lingered in the doorway for what felt like an eternity inside my mind. In reality, it was only a few seconds.

"Yeah, you did say that." I said, trying to conceal the fact that my blood was pumping through my veins in anticipation. *For what? Jasper is off limits! Why do I keep having to remind myself of this?* I could almost taste the memory of his lips in my mind and was grateful when he snapped out of our trance and headed out the door with Lucas in tow. I reached over to give Lucas a quick pat on the head and closed the door behind me before I did something stupid.

Chapter 25

Jasper

Resisting Carla was taking all of my strength. I wanted so badly to be respectful of where she stood in everything, but being with her was like standing in the middle of a candy store without any money. Sure, I could easily steal a piece while no one was watching, but my conscience would eat away at me long before I could let myself taste it…. *So what's the point? Man, I wanted to kiss her so bad, though.*

I let out a sigh of frustration when I entered the stairwell with Lucas. The burst of energy I felt while climbing the remaining 8 flights up to the penthouse was almost supernatural in strength and somehow made the task feel like it was nothing to me. For Lucas, not so much!. "You alright, boy?" I chuckled, as I turned the key to the other entrance of my apartment. It felt so odd using this door, I hadn't opened it in years.

Daylight shined in from the floor to ceiling windows of my living room. I let Lucas off his leash and filled his water bowl. He made quick work of consuming its contents. I realized then, that it would probably be best if I took him with me. He would just have to stay at Silver Linings while I went to go see Sam.

I made a call to Maggie, who surprisingly didn't have all that much for me to do. Apparently, the residents were all pitching in to help Andrew clean up the yard. All she needed from me was to help Andrew retrieve the generators from the attic, so they could power up the kitchen.

"These old shutters did the trick!" Maggie said.

"Well, I'm glad to hear that!" I said. "Listen, would you mind watching Lucas for a bit while I run to the hospital to go see Sam?" I asked.

"Sure, what's wrong with Sam?" She asked.

"It's a long story, I'll have to tell you when I get there." I said. "I'll be there in about thirty minutes."

"Okay, sounds good... I'll see you then." She said.

"I'll talk to you later, Bye." I said before hanging up the call.

~

When I arrived at the office, I could see why everyone was happy to help Andrew outside in the yard. It was so hot and stuffy inside. Maggie was sitting behind the front desk managing the phone lines. I told her about the situation that happened at the club with Sam.

142

"You're kidding me. Weren't you there too?" She asked.

"No, I was at the lake house." I almost forgot that Maggie didn't know about the situation with Sam and Lena and this baby and I didn't feel like digging into it all right now.

"Well, I'm glad you weren't there and it sounds like Sam is going to be okay. I wonder what that was all about though. Do you have any idea?"

"No... but I'm definitely gonna find out." I combed my fingers through my hair trying to come up with something to deflect the conversation. "So, you said the generators are up in the attic?" I asked, hoping she would take the bait.

"Yes. In the resident house." She replied. I can call Andrew on the radio to come help you. Oh, and don't worry about the shutters, we can leave that for tomorrow."

"Are you sure?" I asked. I was relieved because I knew that job was going to take all day, if not longer.

"Yes. Go see Sam and wish him well for me, will ya? I'll tell Andrew to meet you over by the attic." She said. In all honesty, I wasn't really looking forward to seeing Sam, but my conscience was really beginning to eat at me for holding onto this secret I had been keeping from him. I knew it was time to confess. I couldn't keep hiding from him anymore. I could only be honest and say what I needed to, in hopes he might forgive me.

"Alright," I said as I turned to walk out. "You're sure it's okay to leave

Lucas here for a bit?" I asked.

"Yes. Go! Everyone's been working out in the yard, all morning, I'm sure they're all starving by now!" She laughed.

"I'm going!" I flashed her a quick smile. "Thanks!" I said as I left for the resident house.

Andrew and I got the generators down from the attic and up and running for Maggie, so the kitchen staff could get to work on fixing lunch for everyone. The residents were more than excited to keep Lucas entertained until I got back. After seeing how happy Lucas seemed to be with all the attention he was given, I left for the hospital.

Chapter 26

⚜

The emergency room was a crowded mess. People were lined up to see the triage nurse and many patients were in beds out in the hallway because there weren't any rooms left for them to be assigned to. The whole place reeked of alcohol and iodine. I soon had about enough of it.

I moved past the line and found the front desk, where I had to present my license. I had to take my photo for an access sticker to wear on my shirt. I was then directed across the bridge to the other side of the hospital, where I took the elevator up to the 6th floor and followed the numbers on the wall to find the room that Sam had been assigned to.

I took a deep breath to brace myself, in the case that Lena was there with him. She was the last person I wanted to see right now. I took a peek inside the window before opening the door. I was surprised to find him laying there alone in his bed, half asleep.

"Knock, knock." I said, as I walked through the door.

Sam looked up at me and gave me a half lidded smile. "Hey." He said.

"Hey champ, how ya holding up?" I asked.

Sam pressed the button on his bed controller to lift it into to a seated position. "Not too bad, they have me all jacked up on pain meds." He replied with a groan. "I think they're starting to wear off now."

A welcome burst of cool air hit me from the vent above my head as I took a seat in the chair next to Sam's bed. After my hike across the hospital, it felt nice to finally have some a/c, but it did nothing for the tightness that was seeping into my chest. The sudden realization hit me that I could no longer keep this secret from Sam as I watched him lying there in agony. I couldn't escape the thought that he could have died before I ever had the chance to man up about things.

"Listen bud. There's something I have been meaning to talk to you about." I bit out before I lost my courage to come clean. I cleared my throat. "You're not gonna like what I have to tell you." I started to say when the door to Sam's room swung open. Sam and I were both startled by a rather abrupt entrance of his nurse.

"What's your pain level? Are you ready for your meds?" The nurse asked Sam, barging right in the middle of our conversation. She was clearly hyped up on caffeine or cocaine, one of the two.

"Could you give us a minute, please?" Sam asked the nurse.

"Sure. Things are pretty hectic around here, but I'll be back in a little while." She said. Just as quick as she came in, she was gone. Sam's eyes were on the door until it closed, then he turned his gaze to me.

"As I was saying…" *Why was this so hard?* I wondered while swallowing the lump that formed inside my throat. I tried to continue. "I… uh."

"Wait!" Sam interrupted me. "I know what you're gonna say. Please don't." He said.

"What do you mean?" I asked.

Sam looked like he was struggling to find his own words when he let out a sharp exhale in frustration. "The baby is mine." He said. "I know… you think it's yours, but it's not." *What the fuck?* "How do you know that? Did Lena tell you?" I asked, as my head began to spin in all directions. I was so angry at Lena and frustrated for Sam.

"No. The truth is… well, the truth is, you're probably going to hate me for everything I have to tell you, but I can't keep going this way." Sam shifted in his bed, as he tried to get comfortable. "Someone is gonna get hurt! Lena might be in trouble. I haven't been able to reach her since the shooting… I've gotta find her, but I'm stuck in this Goddamn hospital bed!"

"What are you talking about?" I asked. Sam wasn't making any sense.

"The whole baby thing was a dumb plan. She is pregnant, but it's my child, not yours. And now she might be in danger. The check she was asking you for was for me." Sam confessed. "I fucked up, Jasper." Sam's eyes drifted for a moment before he narrowed in on me again.. "Big time. I thought this whole night club was the solution to help me out of it… but these people are really fucking crazy! They're the ones who fucking shot me!" Sam genuinely looked scared, but I still didn't understand what the hell he was talking about.

147

"I don't understand. How did I get involved with this whole baby thing? And what did you do to fuck things up?" I needed to know now, for my own sanity, before I lost i on Sam.

"I fucking lost a shit ton of money at this underground casino in NY. It's run by some Russian mob. They extended me a line of credit and now I owe them a shit ton of money. They've been following me, and I couldn't get them their money fast enough. Lena came up with a plan to spike your drink and let you believe that this baby was yours so she could get you to give her that check."

There it all was, laid out on the table for me, like a good swift kick to my gut! I couldn't believe Sam even had the balls to confess all of that to me. I had to get out of this room before I punched him square in the face.

"Excuse me." I said, before taking a sharp inhale of breath as stood up to leave.

"Wait! There's more. Where are you going?" Sam cried out to me. "I know I'm an asshole, but I am sorry. Please... say something. Say anything! I need your help, Jasper!"

"I can't even look at you right now, Sam! I need a minute." I said as I walked out the door. I was so angry at Sam, I could barely even breathe, my adrenaline was so high. *How could he do this to me?*

~

I don't think I had ever felt so betrayed in my entire life. I paced the halls of the hospital to try and calm myself down. It took every bit of strength I had in me to utilize the tactic I had learned in anger management of stepping outside of my anger.

After some time, the realization hit me. Although I hadn't seen this coming from someone I considered to be my brother, one fact remained... I was *not* the father of Lena's baby. This was my ticket to winning Carla's love back, if she would still have me. It was one hell of a trade off, and the only one I would even consider worth the headache I had been through over this past month. *I could have my Angel back!* If only I could convince her that this crazy storm of mine was truly gone for good. I let my mind fixate on the sheer joy of having this knowledge and let it slowly seep in to take the place of my anger. Soon the blood that ran hot inside my veins had finally cooled off.

The truth was, Sam didn't stand a chance without my help. And even though I was spitting mad at him, I understood the desperate situation he was in is that brought him to betray me the way he did. In all honesty, if it weren't for Sam's guidance in the stock market when I received my inheritance, I wouldn't even be in the position to help him out in the way he needed me to. I had to give him credit for coming clean with me.

I couldn't wait to share this news with Carla. I sent her a text message, asking her to meet me at the park at 7. I looked at my watch to find it was almost four o'clock. I still had to go pick Lucas up and get home in time to meet up with Carla if she agreed to meet me. As for Sam, I would have to come up with a plan to help him out, but I wasn't letting him off the hook so easily. He was going to learn from this situation he put himself in and I was going to make sure he got the help he needed.

I found my way back to Sam's room and waited in the hallway while the nurse gave him his meds. As soon as she left the room, I went inside.

"You need to tell me everything, Sam. And I mean, everything!" I said as I walked through the door. This time, I wasn't sitting down.

"Look man. I'm sorry. Everything spun off so quickly, I just lost control." Sam said.

"I still can't wrap my head around the fact that you gambled away $2 million fucking dollars. How could you be so irresponsible?" I asked.

"$2 million dollars?" Sam asked, scratching his head as if he were confused.

"That's how much Lena told me to write the check for."

"I've been paying them off every week with my share of returns from the club. I still owe them just over 5 hundred grand. She was only supposed to ask for $1 million. I don't know why she told you $2 million. Jesus! I wasn't trying to bleed you dry, man. I just needed enough to get myself out of this jam and enough to get us a place to live so we could finally get out of that crappy motel we're in."

Sam went on to tell me about how his gambling addiction started after he took a big hit in the stock market and how he met Lena at one of the high stakes poker games he was in. His plan started off with good intentions, but he wasn't making the money fast enough for the mob, who obviously took their money matters very seriously.

"So what's the situation with Lena? Why is she in trouble?" I asked.

Sam took a deep breath. "Okay, so... Lena is a prostitute. Well, not by choice. She was trafficked in by the same Russian mob who controls the casino. She wasn't supposed to leave. Now they want her back and I haven't heard anything from her since the shooting." Sam said as his eyes began to pool with tears. I hadn't seen Sam cry since we were teenagers. "You should hear the things she's been through, man. I couldn't stand to hear it. I made her stop telling me, when she did. I had to get her out of there, Jasper!" This explained a lot about Lena.

"Did I even sleep with Lena in the first place?" I asked. I wanted to know everything.

Sam swallowed hard. "No. It was all staged. All she did was drive your car back to our place after we spiked your drink. I followed her to help get you inside and onto the bed, then took off before you woke up to make it seem like the two of you ran off together." Sam's guilt was eating him alive, it was plain to see in his expression. "I know. It was a dumb move. In theory, it was a great plan... for someone who didn't have a conscience about stabbing their best friend in the back. I should never have let her talk me into it but I didn't know what else to do."

"How about the truth, Sam?" I asked in a furious tone as my anger began to resurface.

"Did you ever even think to just come right out and ask me to help you?"

"I don't know, man. I was embarrassed. You're right. I should have just come to you. I am sorry. You've gotta help me find her, Jasper. She's pregnant with my baby. Please." Sam pleaded.

"I will wire you the funds to pay off your debt. You're gonna sign over your half of the club to me to make up for it and I'm gonna sell it. It was never really my dream anyway, it was yours. As for Lena, you're on your own with that mess!" I felt for Sam, I truly did, but he really did me dirty on this one. I would probably never fully trust him ever again. As for Lena, I was far too angry with what she did to go chasing after her.

"I appreciate your help, man. I'll go find Lena on my own when I get out of here, I guess." Sam said in an exhale of breath chocked full of relief from the stress he was under.

"You're also going to get some help for your gambling addiction or you may as well lose my number entirely." I added. "I'll talk to Maggie. I'm sure she'll know where to go for help. I gotta go. I'll be in touch after I talk to Maggie."

Chapter 27

Carla

The stagnant air inside the apartment made it impossible to relax. After Jasper left, I went back out on the terrace to sit with Jamie and Dillon. They started talking about what happened to Eddie. I was so glad they didn't mention it while Jasper was here and I damn sure wasn't gonna be the one to tell them that it was Jasper who knocked him out. The last thing I needed was to cause any more friction for Jasper. Instead, I played dumb. I had planned on telling Jamie what really happened, but not until Dillon was gone. It wasn't like he Dillon seemed the type to cause trouble, but I'd been sorely wrong in the past. I never would have dreamed that AJ would've went to the lengths he did with me and Abby.

"Did he get a look at who it was?" I asked, trying to fish for information.

"No. We were hoping you might know." Dillon replied. "He said one minute he was keeping a watch on you, and the next minute everything went black."

"We were both out on the dance floor. Neither of us actually saw what happened." Jamie added.

"Oh." I said, putting on my best poker face. "That's too bad." I hated lying, but I didn't know how else to handle the situation. Especially without knowing how Dillon might react if he found out it was Jasper. "Well, I think I might try to go lay down for a little bit and get some reading in. It's been a long weekend." I said, trying to escape having to lie any more than I already had.

"It's way too stuffy inside for me, I don't know how you can stand it. I hope they get the power back on soon." Jamie said as I stood up to go inside.

"Me too, but I'm gonna try." I agreed before retreating to my bedroom. I opened the window to let some fresh air inside and laid down on my bed. I grabbed the book from off of my nightstand and read a few chapters before I fell asleep.

~

I was walking by the shore with Jasper when out of nowhere, the sky turned dark. The wind carried a sense of danger as the clouds seeped low into the horizon and began to form a cyclonic force. It was so magnificent to watch, we were both stunned still, until it began heading in our direction.

Jasper quickly took my hand as we both made a run for cover. We were running so fast, I could barely keep up, but Jasper never let go of my hand. We finally made it to shelter inside the exterior cellar of an old abandoned house.

It was so dark inside, we could barely see each other. Jasper held me close against his chest as we listened to what had to be golf ball sized hail pounding on the cellar door. I was so scared. The pounding only lasted a few minutes, but it felt like it went on forever. I'd never been in a tornado before. I leaned into listen to the beating of Jasper's heart, and instantly felt a sense of calmness wash over me. We may have had disaster beating at the cellar door, but with him, I felt like I was safe at home.

When the sound of the hail began to quiet, Jasper reached above our heads to lift the cellar door. He took a peek outside and quickly slammed it shut. The twister was tearing up the house and heading straight for us.

"I'm scared, Jasper!" I cried.

"Don't worry, Angel. We're gonna be okay. We just have to wait it out a little while longer until it passes." Jasper said as he pulled me back into his arms again. I started to hum to ease my mind from worry. A lullaby Mama used to sing to me when I was little.

A few minutes later, everything got quiet. We waited a few more minutes before Jasper lifted the cellar door again. This time, the storm was gone. We stepped outside to find the old abandoned house in complete shambles, but we were both safe. Phew!

As we walked past the rubble, it suddenly took on a life force of its own, like magic. Soon Jasper and I were surrounded by a large swarm of dragonflies. They circled around us for a period before disappearing into the sky.

The sun was beginning to set when I woke up from my dream. I took my phone off the nightstand and went out into the living room. The power was still off and there was no sign of Jamie or Dillon. I stepped out on the terrace to call Jamie when I noticed a text message had come through from Jasper.

Jasper:

I need to see you. Can you meet me at the park at 7?

It sounded urgent, but it was already almost 7 o'clock and I was in no way, shape or form, ready to see him. Not to mention the fact that the elevators were still down because we didn't have power. *Why did it even matter how I looked?* I wondered as I ran inside to catch a glimpse of myself in the mirror that hung on the dining room wall. I would at least need to get a quick shower. A cold one, in the dark, at that! I had to remind myself.

Me:

How about 7:30? Jasper quickly texted me back.

Jasper:

That's perfect. I'm just pulling in now. Do we have power yet?

Me:

Negative

Jasper:

Are you hungry? Have you had dinner yet?

Me:

I haven't eaten all day, I just woke up.

Jasper:

I'm gonna take Lucas out and see if anything's open. Stay put for now. I'll text you soon.

Me:

Okay

I forgot to ask Jamie where she put the hurricane supplies, so I took the candle Jasper bought me into the bathroom and lit it so I could see. I turned on the shower, hoping it would magically turn warm, but it didn't. Ice freaking cold! Needless to say, that shower was short lived.

I stepped out of the shower and a chill hit me, giving me goosebumps. I quickly put on my robe to warm myself up. When I opened the door, it was evident that what was left of daylight was quickly diminishing throughout our apartment, so I brought the candle with me to my bedroom so I could see. I couldn't imagine what Jasper wanted to talk to me about. We had just spent the entire weekend together at his lake house.

As I rummaged through my closet, looking for something to wear, I noticed the temperature inside my bedroom had dropped significantly with the setting of the sun. It was actually beginning to feel chilly with the breeze coming in through the window. Surely, the cold shower was no help! I threw on a tank top, and draped my over sized burnt orange cable knit sweater over my shoulders. I paired it with some black leggings and my favorite pair of black boots. I was dressed in the definition of fall and cozy.

By now, the apartment had turned completely dark, so I went outside on the patio to wait for Jasper's call. It was Jamie who called me first.

"Hello?" I asked.

"Hey! Is the power back on yet?"

"No, not yet." I replied. "Where are you?"

"Well that figures…You were sleeping when we left, so I didn't want to wake you. We went out to find something to eat. We're having dinner at the Chinese place, since we had pizza last night. Do you want us to bring you something home?" She asked.

"Actually, I think I might be having dinner with Jasper. I'm waiting to hear back from him now." I replied, just as I heard a knock on the front door. "Hold on, Jamie… Someone's at the door. Are you expecting someone?" I asked.

"No." She replied.

"I opened the door to find Jasper and Lucas standing in the doorway. The aroma of the pizza pie he had resting on his shoulder hit me with the sudden realization of just how famished I really was.

"Jasper's here now." I said. "Looks like we're having pizza." I said to Jamie on the phone.

"Okay." She said. "So I guess I'll be seeing you some time tomorrow then." She laughed.

"I'll text you later, okay." I nearly whispered as if Jasper could hear what she said to me. I was beginning to blush from Jamie's insinuation.

"Bye!" Jamie said, cheerfully.

"OK, bye!" I said, before ending the call with Jamie..

"Hey Angel," Jasper said as he remained in the hallway with Lucas. "You're never gonna believe what I have to tell you." The lights began to flicker inside the apartment.

"The power! It's back on!" I shouted, as the flickering stopped and the lights remained.

"That would've been awesome 7 flights ago!" Jasper chuckled with a flash of his dimple. My stomach took a dive at the mere sight before me.

"Why don't you two come inside and rest a minute?" I said, taking notice of Lucas and his panting.

"Thanks." Jasper said as he and Lucas entered the apartment. Jasper set the pizza down on the dining room table, while I went into the kitchen to fetch a bowl of water for Lucas.

"Well, at least we won't have to take the stairs again." Jasper said as he set the pizza box down and took a seat at the dining room table.

"That pizza smells so good. Should I grab us some plates?" I asked.

"Sure. We can eat now if you want." Jasper agreed. We sat at the table eating our pizza while Lucas slurped up every bit of water in his bowl.

"Poor Lucas" I giggled.

"You should have seen me trying to make it up the stairs without dropping the pizza. It almost didn't make it here in one piece." Jasper laughed as he took a bite of his slice.

"So, what did you want to tell me?" I wondered. Jasper went on to tell me what Sam had confessed to him.

"Wow." I was in complete shock! More at the fact that Sam had the guts to come clean with Jasper, than anything else. I had the sense that something sinister was going on with those two all along.

"I know. I was so mad, I had to leave." Jasper said.

"That's insane! I can't believe they drugged you. And now Lena is missing too? Is she really pregnant?"I was dying to know!"

"Oh, she's pregnant alright." Jasper's eyes began to sparkle with his smile. "That baby is Sam's, not mine. Everything was staged. I never even slept with her!"

"Hold crap! So what are you gonna do?" I asked.

"I have to help him. They barely missed him this time... next time, he might not be so lucky." Jasper paused to consider his next words. "Honestly, if it weren't for Sam, I wouldn't even be in the position to help him at all. He's the one who helped me with my investments in the stock market." Jasper confessed.

"I suppose that makes sense." I said as the front door swung open, abruptly.

"Thank God! The power is back!" Jamie cried. Lucas was startled and quickly started barking at Jamie and Dillon when they walked through the door.

"Well, I better get him upstairs." Jasper said, as he tightened his grip on Lucas's leash. Jamie looked frightened.

"Don't worry. He's harmless. All bark, no bite!" Jasper reassured Jamie. "Wanna come with me?" Jasper asked with a smile I could never say no to.

"Sure! I'll grab the pizza." I said. I was more than ready for another slice.

Chapter 28

W e took the elevator up to Jasper's penthouse. Jasper freed Lucas from his leash. I walked over to the kitchen island and set the pizza box down on the kitchen island.

"Well, I'm a sweaty mess. I'm going to run upstairs and get a shower." Jasper turned to me and said before setting Lucas's leash on the counter next to the pizza box.

"Okay. Would you mind if I have another slice?" I asked, shyly.

"You don't have to ask, silly girl." Jasper laughed, as he casually stepped in behind me to reach for a glass above my head. When his body brushed up against mine, ever so slightly, I felt an instant flash of tingles run through me."How about a glass of wine to go with your pizza?" He asked. *How could I say no?* After getting a whiff of the pheromones radiating from his perspiration, I knew I would need something to settle my nerves.

I caught myself staring at every move Jasper made when he opened the bottle of Chianti and poured us each a glass. "Wine sounds good." I quickly agreed, swallowing the lump that had formed inside my throat.

"I won't be long., I promise." He said before handing me my glass. The tone of his voice was deep and guttural. "Make yourself at home, Angel." *Angel!*

I took a sip of wine and watched him walk up the stairs to his loft. My appetite suddenly escaped into the abyss of my lusty thoughts, but I knew I needed to eat. I forced myself to finish my other slice then took my glass of wine over to the sofa to sit down. Lucas was sprawled out in front of the couch, on the cold floor, panting away.

As I sat there sipping on my wine, I began to process everything Jasper had revealed to me before we came upstairs. I knew Lena was dangerous, I felt it in her energy the very first time I saw her. I couldn't even begin to imagine the life she must have had to endure to bring her to the darkness she was surrounded by. A life of survival at the greasy hands of dirty men just might do it. *But what about Sam? How could he deceive his own best friend, like that?* I guess that old saying is true. Desperate times call for desperate measures. Still, I didn't think I could ever bring myself to do that to someone I claimed to love. Then again, I've never been in the position to be faced with that sort of decision.

One fact rang true through of all of this. If this baby truly was Sam's and not Jasper's, it changed everything. It meant Lena was out of the picture and Jasper was no longer off limits! *We could finally be together!* I let myself settle into this realization while Jasper made his way back down the stairs. He joined me on the couch with his own glass of wine.

"Care for another glass?" He asked, taking notice that I had almost finished the one I was drinking.

"Um... sure." I replied.

"So, what are your plans for Halloween?" Jasper asked, while pouring me another glass of wine.

"Oh, right... that's tomorrow, isn't it?" Between the storm and everything else going on, I nearly forgot. "Jamie and I vaguely discussed watching horror movies and passing out candy to trick or treators, but we never actually confirmed it. I think Dillon might be staying over though, so he might be there too. Do you want to come over?" I asked, hoping the small talk between us might convince the butterflies to keep their dance inside my belly at a minimum.

"Sure. I haven't done that in years." Jasper replied with a chuckle. The dimple shining through his smile quickly swayed them back into their rhythm. I took another large sip of my wine.

"You alright, Angel?" Jasper asked, taking notice of my unease. *Shit! Was I that obvious?* I shifted in my seat and looked away.

"I'm-" I hummed out in an attempt to tell him I was fine, but he quickly stifled my words with a kiss. The sweet flavor of wine on his tongue only made me want to taste him even more.

"Shit! I'm sorry." Jasper pulled away and combed his fingers through his wet hair. *No, don't stop, please!* I could swear he heard my thoughts, when he quickly retracted his decision and pulled me closer, within his grip. "Okay, I'm not sorry. I can't take it anymore, Angel." He whispered before locking his lips with mine again.

The current flowing between us was more than palpable and damn near impossible to resist. I couldn't blame him any more than I could blame myself. It was as if we'd both climbed a mountain from opposite ends and found each other at its peak, in our discovery of the truth. We both wanted this so badly we could taste it! Every sense we had was screaming at us to give in to the temptation of this powerfully magnetic force that was our love. Our resistance to one another had become a faded memory we could barely remember. We both knew, there was no escaping our desire for each other any longer.

"Come with me." Jasper breathed before taking my glass of wine and setting it down on the table next to his. He took my hand and led me up the stairs to his loft, where we both relinquished our restrain to this uninhibited force between us.

Before I knew it, we were both completely naked at his bed with a trail of our clothing leading behind us. The only thing I could see was the fire behind his sapphire gaze when he coaxed me into the navy blue satin sheets of his bed. The silky soft texture against my bare skin had me feeling like a goddess, lying in wait.

Jasper hovered over me, smoothing his hands over my shoulders down to my hands as he stretched them out, above my head. "My beautiful Angel." He whispered in my ear. "So beautiful." He said, trailing kisses down my neck before claiming my lips with his own. Every sense inside me, on high alert, anticipating his next move. Boy, did he deliver! I felt the slightly calloused texture of his palms smooth over my naked breasts as he trickled his fingers down to my rib cage. He paused at the center of my abdomen, before pushing me back a little further onto the bed, allowing him the access he desired.

"I have waited so long for this." He breathed over my belly as the butterflies within me danced in delight to his words. He beveled his fingers across to my hips at both sides as they found there way up under my rear. Jasper kneeled down to his knees at the foot of his bed and plunged his mouth over my clitoris, where he began sucking in full force as if he craved my taste with everything he had. I could feel the fire raging within him with every movement he made. I couldn't help myself from crying out his name. "Jasper!"

Hearing my voice only fueled his burning desire, as he dug his fingers into the flesh of my rear, pulling me further into his mouth. "You taste so sweet, Angel" he breathed. "Don't stop!" I selfishly moaned out in delight as my body begin to quiver from his detachment. I combed my fingers through the moist waves of his freshly washed hair and gently guided him back.

He quickly obliged, working his fingers in and out of me while sliding his tongue up and down, until I could take no more. I wanted him inside me so bad, I could taste it.

Jasper, please!" I begged as I pulled his head up to see the longing my eyes.

"Say no more, Angel, all you ever have to do is ask." Jasper said as he reached over to grab a condom.

He slowly pushed himself inside me and began working us into rhythm we could both latch on to. For the first time in over a month, I felt whole. Having him inside me was like a key to a world of magic, where everything seemed to make sense. Suddenly, it hit me… He was what I had been missing this entire time. It didn't take either of us very long to find our release because we had both gone far too long without.

We spent the rest of the night lying in bed, wrapped in each other's warmth, cherishing the treasure we had both rediscovered in each other as we made love, over and over again until we could no more.

Chapter 29

A wakened by the golden rays of the morning sun, dancing through the blinds of Jasper's bedroom window, the bed beneath me felt cool and soft against my skin as I took in a breath of the sweet air around me. I heard the sound of the shower faucet cease and the curtain slide open from inside the bathroom. I turned to my attention to the doorway. to find a dripping, wet Jasper, wearing nothing but a periwinkle, blue towel draped around his waist. I damn near lost my breath when he shook his head. The tiny droplets of water spewed all around him, illuminating every glistening curve of his upper torso when he stepped out onto the carpeted floor of his bedroom. I was far too comfy to get out of bed.

"Good morning, Angel." He said.

"Hi." I replied, shyly as I watched him come towards the bed to sit down next to me. The intoxicating scent, radiating from his skin, swept me away to a place where all I could think about were the places he took my mind, body and soul to the night before.

"I wish I could stay in bed with you all morning." He said, as he peered deep into the longing, far from being hidden, behind my eyes.

"Me too. I don't have to work at the coffee shop today." I agreed, with a suggestive smile.

"Unfortunately, I've got a ton of work to do for Maggie." He sighed, swiping his finger tip along the button of my nose. "You should go back to sleep, Angel. Stay as long as you like." He added. He leaned over, pressing his lips to my forehead, before standing up to get dressed. I had to admit his suggestion did sound rather enticing as I rolled over into his pillow. I could have easily laid there, dreaming about us all morning.

"If it takes as long to get the shutters off as it took put them on, I'll probably be seeing you later at the office." He chuckled, while pulling on his shirt.

"Well, I hope it doesn't give you too much trouble, but I'd really love to see you again." I said as I watched him exit his bedroom to head downstairs.

Chapter 30

Halloween 2012

Sam

After being released from the hospital, I took an Uber over to Club Hush to get my car. Lena hadn't answered or returned any of my calls since the night I got shot. *Where was she?* I knew it was a gamble, going back to the motel we were staying at, but I still had hopes of finding her there. *No such Luck!* Everything looked the same as it had when we left together, the night everything went down at the club.

I plugged my phone into the wall to charge it and went down the hallway to grab a soda from the vending machine. When I got back, my phone had enough battery for me to turn it on while it was plugged to use it. I logged into my bank account app to find that Jasper kept his word and wired the funds into my account. *Man, I really owe him for this one.* I wasn't giving those bastards one red cent. Not until I found Lena. It was the only leverage I had in getting her back!

I knew it was a lost cause, but I dialed her number again just to see if she might answer. It rang twice before I heard a foreign man's voice pick up the call.

"Sam?" He asked.

"Who is this?" I quickly asked, as all the blood rushed to my head.

"This is Dimitri. I am Lena's brother." He replied.

"Where's Lena? Why do you have her phone?" This can't be good. She told me all about her brother and his connection to the men that were keeping her trapped in that shitty life of prostitution.

"She's in the hospital, Sam." *No! What's happened? Did they shoot her too?* I had a million thoughts flying through my mind. None of them were good.

"She's going to be okay." Dimitri replied in his heavy Russian accent. " She told me you would call. She wanted me to tell you. Her water broke. I think she might lose baby."

"Where is she, Dimitri? Which hospital?" I asked, rushing to my feet.

"We are in Philadelphia. I will take you to her when you get here. Can you come here? he asked."I need your help, Sam. She told me you would help me."

"Help you with what?" I didn't understand what he was talking about.

"I'll explain everything when you get here." He said before giving me the address of where to meet him. "I'm counting on you, Sam. Please hurry." He added before ending the call.

Something told me that this was my only chance at getting Lena back. I didn't have time to wonder whether I could trust Dimitri. I knew I had to act fast! I quickly packed a bag with some clothes and essentials and took off for the address he gave me.

~

Jasper

I was drenched in sweat. The blazing, hot sun was beating down on my back. These old screws were giving me hell on the last few boards that needed to be removed from the windows of the old mansion. Surprisingly, with Andrew's help, we actually made better time than I imagined it would take.

I had just climbed down the ladder when I got the call from Sam. I dug my sweaty hands into my back pocket to retrieve my phone when I noticed Carla pull into the drive.

"Hello?" I said, answering Sam's call.

"Jasper! Thank God! You answered." Sam said. His tone was urgent. "Listen. I know I owe you my life, but I need another favor. By the way, I got the funds you sent, thank you."

"What do you want, Sam?" I asked, annoyed. I didn't want any more reminders or apologies or thank you's. All I wanted was for Sam to

172

get his shit together. If he had the balls to call me to ask for anything else, it must have been detrimental.

"This isn't for me. I mean, it is, but it isn't." Sam stumbled out.

"On with it, Sam. I don't have time for this." I said. I made eye contact with Carla who was headed for the office. She gave me a wave before walking inside.

"Listen... I need you to come meet me here in Philadelphia. I'm on my way over to see Lena. Her brother, Dimitri, will be here, in case I'm not back." Sam bit out. "There are seven girls here. They all need a safe place to stay. At least for a few days, until we can figure things out for them. Is there any room at Silver Linings? You gotta find out for me." Sam sounded desperate.

"Why is Lena in the hospital? What the fuck have you gotten yourself into now?" I asked.

"I don't have time to explain. I didn't have time to charge my phone. Lena's water broke. She might lose the baby, Jasper. That's all I know. I'm on my way to go see her now to find out what's going on." Sam was on the verge of tears, I could hear it in his voice. "You have to trust me, Jasper, please! These girls, they need your help! Please just say you'll come and I will text you the address."

"I need to know what the fuck I'm walking into here, Sam." I replied.

"Dimitri isn't a threat! But you may want to bring some protection, just in case."

"I'll be there. You have my word. Text me the address." I replied, before ending the call.

"I have an emergency, I have to go. I'll be back tomorrow to help you clean this up." I said to Andrew, motioning to the pile of boards that were sprawled out in the yard.

"Don't worry about that, I'll take care of it. I'll get Tony to help me later this evening." Andrew said. "Go handle your business. You've been a great help!"

"Thanks, man. If not, there's a tarp out in the shed. You can just stack them and cover it up, until tomorrow when I get back." I said.

"Okay." Andrew replied as he set out to find the tarp inside the shed. I rinsed myself off with the hose and headed inside the office to go find Maggie.

~

Carla was on the phone when I stepped inside the office. I gave her a wave as I walked passed her desk and down the hallway to Maggie's office. Her office door was closed, so I knocked.

"Come in." She called out from inside. Maggie was talking on the phone when I walked inside her office.

"I hate to interrupt, but I need to ask you something really quick." I said. She signaled a finger to me to wait while she asked the person she was talking to to hold the line.

"What's up, Jasper?" She asked.

"We finished taking down all the boards. I have to go meet Sam in Philly, so I'll be gone the rest of the day. Do you have space for seven girls? Sam says they need a safe place to stay."

"We only have three rooms left, one of them will likely be going to the person I'm talking to now, so that will only leave me with two. What's the deal? Are they minors?"

"I honestly don't know. I'll find out more when I see Sam. He didn't have time to tell me. He just said it was urgent." I replied.

"Right now, I would only have room for four." She replied. "We have a few intakes coming in from the storm, but we also have a couple rooms opening up in the next few weeks." She replied.

"Alright. Hold those rooms for me, please." I said. "I have to get home and get a shower before I leave."

"Okay, thanks for all your help, Jasper. I don't know what we would do without you." Maggie smiled. "Keep me posted on the girls, please." She said before returning to the call she was on.

I walked back towards Carla's desk. I had to let her know I wouldn't be able to make it for our Halloween plans. I hated to let her down, but Sam sounded serious. Even though I was still pissed at him about everything, he was still my brother. I couldn't bring myself to let him down.

Chapter 31

Carla

I felt Jasper's energy moving towards me as he walked down the hall. The moment the image of his face flashed through my mind, he was right there in front of my desk.

"Hey Angel. I'm sorry to do this to you at the last minute, but I'm afraid I won't be able to make it tonight." He said, stealing away the magic I felt, as if he were ripping the band aid off a fresh wound.

"Oh?" I asked, urging him to explain with my eyes.

"Sam needs me to meet him out in Philadelphia." His purposeful gaze gave me a chance to get a good read on the sincerity shining through his eyes. "Lena's in the hospital. Sam thinks she might lose the baby. Apparently, he needs me to find a safe place for some girls who are in trouble.

"Oh... Wow, OK!" I said. That was a lot to take in, a curve ball I wasn't expecting. "It sounds to me like Sam's got his hands full, right now. Please let him and Lena know that I will be praying for them and the baby." I was sad that Jasper couldn't make our plans for Halloween, but I wanted to be mature about it. And while my thoughts about Sam and Lena were rather indifferent after everything that went down, I knew that Sam was still Jasper's best friend and this was his baby's life at stake.

"I will. Maggie doesn't have room for all of them yet. I was wondering if you could do me a favor if you've got some time to spare?" He asked, while reaching into the pocket of his jeans for his wallet. He pulled out a credit card and placed it on the desk in front of me.

"Sure, what do you need?" I asked, eager to help out in any way that I could.

"I wanted to do this together, but I trust you. Can you look online for some furniture for the lake house?" He asked. "I may have to let these girls stay there for a little while. I want to make sure they'll have whatever they need. I'm mostly concerned about the beds, so just pay whatever it costs to have them delivered there soon as possible and I'll put them together when I can."

"You're letting them stay there?" I asked. I was shocked that he would open up his home to complete strangers.

"For now it's just a back up plan. I'll have to assess the situation when I meet them, obviously, but I want to be prepared, in case I do decide to let them stay there temporarily until more rooms open up here."

"I don't know, Jasper." I replied, nervously running my fingers through my hair. "What if you hate what I pick out?" I asked. I didn't want to let him down. Jasper came over to my side of the desk and rested his hands on my shoulder. My heart skipped a beat at his touch.

"You can do me no wrong, Angel. I promise. I bought this house for *us*. It was always my plan for you to make it a place you will love. I trust you." He said, reassuringly. "I have to go so I can get cleaned up before I leave. Buy anything you see, that you like. If you love it, I promise you, I will love it too. This card has more than enough to cover anything you find." He said, lifting my chin to plant me with an electrifying kiss to remember. The kind that made me momentarily forget where I was. "I don't know how long I'll be gone, but I will be in touch."

"Okay. I'll see what I can find." I said, reassuring him that I was up for the task. I watched him walk out the front door of the office and tucked his credit card into the outside pocket of my purse.

The energy he left me with in his departure empowered me. I felt confident in his trust. I quickly began my quest of shopping online to furnish the lake house. I put a lot of thought into the memory of what the place looked like and tried my best to find things I thought would suit it well. I loaded things that I would like and hoped he would too in the cart. Before I knew it, I had beds for all the bedrooms, living room furniture and a table for the dining room, all being delivered within the next 2 days, with priority fees for expedited delivery.

After spending more than a few nights in Jasper's bed, I had a pretty good idea of what his taste might be in terms of quality and went with all white sheets and feather down comforters for all the beds. A neutral color scheme of earth tones, white and navy blue dressings would compliment the nautical style of the house.

The solid oak dining table was my favorite of all the furniture pieces. It had convertible, hidden storage with extra stools and a leaf to extend the table when needed. I imagined Jasper would likely set the table with fresh flowers, just like he did in our office. I was excited when I found the beautiful daffodil and white lace cloth napkins to dress the stone white dinnerware for the table. Everything was coming together so nicely.

Friday was the earliest day they had available for delivery on the living room set, but once I found it, I knew that it was perfect! It was made of soft white leather, just like the one in Jasper's penthouse, only this one was a wrap-around sectional with built-in recliners at each end. It came equipped with built-in storage ottomans that could also be used for extra seating in the middle. The sofa would comfortably sit up to eight people and was perfect for lounging around to read or watch movies.

I figured I would let Jasper take over when it came to anything electronic, as I had no clue of what was what, in that department. What I had so far was a good start on what I believed Jasper wanted me to do, but there was still so much more shopping left to do. I had to admit, I was having fun putting everything together for him. When I saw the total, I was a little reluctant, so I sent Jasper a text with the amount to make sure it was okay with him first.

He called me back a few minutes later to give me the go ahead. He told me he had just gotten to the hospital to meet up with Sam to find out what was going on. After we hung up, I went ahead and placed the order for everything, as instructed.

"You're still here?" Maggie startled me as she approached the front desk. I looked up at the time. It was almost 7:30. *Shit!*

"Oh, I'm sorry. I must have gotten a little carried away with what Jasper asked me to do for him." I replied.

"No need to apologize, sweetie." She laughed. "I just figured you might have plans for Halloween."

"You're right, I do." I laughed. "Nothing major. Just watching horror movies and passing out candy with my best friend. I really should get going." I said as I stood up to gather my belongings, and head out the door.

"Sounds like fun. Happy Halloween." Maggie said in my departure.

"Happy Halloween." I called back as I shuffled my way out to my car.

Chapter 32

I didn't hear back from Jasper until 11 o'clock that night. My phone rang just in time to scare the crap out of Jamie, Dillon and me who were all sitting on the couch with our attention on the TV screen, watching Scream. We barely had any trick or treators and it had been hours since the last one knocked on our door.

"It's Jasper." I said to Jamie and Dillon as I hopped off the couch to answer his call. "I'm gonna take this in my bedroom."

"Hello?" I said into the phone.

"Hey… It's me. I was hoping to catch you before you went to bed. We just got back to Boston. I'm at the hotel, getting a room to put the girls in. We had to wait for Lena to be released from the hospital."

"Is everything alright with the baby?" I asked.

"Lena is fine, but the baby isn't going to make it." Jasper sounded tired.

She has to get an abortion because her water broke and the baby won't survive without amniotic fluid." For a moment, I let my heart go out to Lena, imagining how difficult that must have been for her. Then I remembered how she kept threatening to abort the baby anyway.

"I thought you were bringing them over to the lake house." I said.

"That's my back up plan, yes, but I'll need to wait until it's furnished. Did you have any trouble placing the order?" He asked.

"Not at all. I took some screenshots if you want to see them." I replied.

"I trust you, Angel. I'll see them when they get there. How long did they say for delivery?" He asked.

"Everything will be there by Wednesday. The only thing that will take longer is the sofa, and they said that it will be delivered on Friday." I replied.

"Alright, I'll extend the rooms until Thursday for now, so I'll have enough time to put everything together. I'm heading back home after I leave here, but I'm sure you'll be sleeping by then."

"I have to be up at five, so probably." I laughed.

"OK, you should get some sleep. I'll let you go. Good night, Angel." Jasper said.

"You too, get some rest! Good night, Jasper." I said before ending the call. I walked back into the living room to say good night to Jamie and Dillon and went to bed.

As I lay there, I wondered how Jasper could forgive Sam and Lena so easily, after what they did to him. I knew I would eventually come around, but for now, I was still so angry about all of the deception. Jasper was far too smart to play the fool. Perhaps his heart was so big, he sacrificed the sting of his own feelings to see the bigger picture and help them out.

Chapter 33

I t only took a few weeks for the other rooms to open up at Silver
Linings for the girls. I hated being apart from Jasper, in the time
he was away, especially knowing he was around all these girls,
who were literal prostitutes. I knew that wasn't their choice, but I still
wouldn't trust them until I had a chance to meet them myself.

I sensed Jasper knew I was trying my best not to share these thoughts
with him because he made sure to call me every night, while he was
gone. He even came to pick me up so I could spend the weekends there
with him. I couldn't blame him for needing to be there, he didn't know
these girls from Adam.

I felt a lot better once I did finally get the chance to meet the girls. My
jealousy quickly turned to compassion, once I saw how fucked up they
really were about the situation they had come from. They stuck to
each other like a pack of wolves on guard. It was no wonder why they
all chose to stay together, sharing beds at Jasper's lake house, while
they waited for enough rooms to open up at Silver Linings. On my

second weekend visit, I could tell they all seemed to come around and begin to trust Jasper and what he was trying to do for them.

Oddly enough, Lena and Dimitri were a great help. They did most of the cooking and tending to the girls and helped whenever we needed a translator. I saw a complete turn around in Lena's demeanor. She actually seemed quite worried about Sam, when he took off for New York on a mission to pay his debt without getting killed. With the all girls and Dimitri going rogue, Sam knew it was far too risky to even think about bringing Lena with him. He refused to let her come. She still needed to rest from having her abortion, anyway. I was grateful to know, they would all soon receive the help they desperately needed to heal from their trauma, at Silver Linings.

Chapter 34

Thanksgiving Day 2012

I was handing a customer their order when I spotted Lucas through the window of the coffee shop. A moment later, Jasper came trailing up behind him. He tapped on the window and waved at me to come outside. Brooke was already taking care of the only other customer in line.

"I'll be right back." I said to Brooke as I stepped out from behind the counter to meet Jasper outside.

"Hey you." Jasper smiled when I opened the door. Lucas's nub of a tail was wagging away as he whined for me to pet him. I, of course, gave in to his request.

"Hey." I said, brushing my hands off on my apron as I stepped out into the chilly Autumn breeze. "What are you doing here?" I asked.

"We were in the area. I figured I would drop by to deliver some good news." Jasper's eyes twinkled when his smile climbed across to his ears. "Maggie gave you the day off for Thanksgiving!"

"She did?" I asked, stepping in a little closer, so Jasper could block the breeze. I left my jacket inside the shop.

"Yes. Well I asked her to. I'm taking you somewhere, but it's a surprise. What time do you get off?" He asked.

"I should be done in about an hour, as long as we don't get a late rush." I replied. Jasper looked down at his watch.

"That should be perfect! Do you think you can be ready to go by 2 pm?" He asked.

"That depends on what I'm getting ready for." I teased. I wanted him to keep the surprise, but I needed to know how to dress. "Don't tell me what it is, just tell me what should I wear?" I asked.

"Dress comfortably. It's nothing fancy, I promise!" He replied, as I watched him give a tug on Lucas's leash. Lucas was whimpering at a pair of chihuahuas who were crossing the street.

"Well I'm gonna take him for a walk and let you get back to work. I'll pick you up at 2 o'clock." Jasper said as he leaned in to give me a quick peck on the lips, before letting Lucas take the reins. I stood there watching as the two of them headed off towards the park and went back inside to finish my side work.

"So? What did Jasper want?" Brooke asked, curiously when I came back behind the counter.

"He stopped by to let me know that Maggie gave me the day off and that he's taking me somewhere this afternoon." I replied.

"Oh yeah? Where is he taking you?" She asked.

"I don't know, he told me it's a surprise." I said, grinning ear to ear. "He knows how much I love surprises!"

"Well, whatever it is, I hope you guys have fun!" Brooke said. "Jason's mom invited my mom, my grandma and me over for Thanksgiving dinner. I'm sure that's going to be interesting to say the least." She laughed.

"I'll bet!" I agreed. "You'll have to let me know how that goes."

"Oh, I'm sure you'll be hearing all about it tomorrow." She laughed. "Wait until they get a taste of my Grandma's cooking!"

Chapter 35

⟳

"Keep your eyes closed, Angel, or you'll spoil the surprise." Jasper said. I could tell we were turning a corner in his SUV, but I had no idea where we were going.

"They are closed!" I giggled, as I blindly reached for the handle to hold so I could keep my bearings. I still hadn't gotten used to Jasper's love for speed and with my eyes closed, everything felt even more exhilarating.

When we began to slow to a stop, Jasper turned off the ignition and got out on his side of the car. He came around to my side to let me out. We walked down the sidewalk a few minutes, before Jasper put a halt to our steps.

"Hold on here, and give me your other hand. I'll help you up the stairs to the door." He said, placing my hand onto the cold, metal railing. I counted 12 stairs in my head as he guided me up each step, one by one. When we reached the landing of the building we were walking into,

I got a whiff of what I could swear smelled like homemade apple pie. The sudden sound of church bells, chiming loudly in my ear startled me out of balance. Thankfully, Jasper was right there to catch me from falling down the steps we had just climbed up.

"Are you taking me to church?" I asked, as we walked through the door. The space around me felt hollow and dark, but I kept my eyes closed the entire time and continued to count my steps. Wherever we were, I knew I was safe, as long as I was with Jasper. 147 steps in, he finally let go of my hand.

"OK, you can open your eyes now, Angel." He said.

My eyes needed a moment to adjust, as it was darker than I had imagined. There were rows of seating on both sides of us, and a large statue of Jesus Christ on the cross, just above the altar in front of us.

"We *are* in church!" I shouted in a whisper, silently patting myself on my back for guessing correctly. I stood in awe of the beauty I was surrounded by. I'd never been to a church that looked like this before. The ones I went to as a kid never had any statues or beautifully stained glass windows. They were far more simple in their decor, with only a simple cross at the altar.

"Are we the only ones in here?" I asked, as I stood there taking in my surroundings.

"I'm not sure, we are a bit early. Let's go find out." He said, taking my hand in his as we walked passed the altar towards a hallway that led to several doors. Two of the doors were restrooms, another was a utility closet. We walked all the way down to the end of the hallway.

Jasper pushed the door open and we walked inside to find a fairly large kitchen. I was surprised, as it was not at all what I was expecting to see in a church.

"Jasper!" A salt and peppered, gray haired woman wearing a burgundy and cream colored, plaid apron cried out from behind the steel counter where she was busy working. She was surrounded by various fruits and vegetables, she appeared to be prepping. She rinsed her hands off in the sink and came around to give Jasper a great big hug.

"We missed you last year, I didn't think you'd make it!" She said, eyeing me curiously. "Who's the pretty girl?" She asked. I could feel myself blushing at her words.

"This is my..." Jasper hesitated for a beat before continuing. "Linda, this is Carla. She's my girlfriend." He replied, confidently as he wrapped his arm around my waist and pulled me closer.

Linda extended her hand out to shake my hand. "It's so lovely to meet you, dear." She said with a warm and friendly smile. "You caught yourself a good one." She added with a wink.

"It's nice to meet you too." I said, smiling at her remark.

It wasn't very long before the kitchen filled with many more volunteers. They all worked together as a team, preparing a banquet of Thanksgiving dishes. I was tasked with peeling potatoes, while Jasper was in charge of stuffing the turkeys. I couldn't believe how quickly everything had come together. With all the help we had, we had enough food to serve anyone in need, who lined up for a plate. By 6 o'clock, the line of people who were waiting outside to come in, had finally come to an end. Jasper, myself and the rest of the volunteers all joined our remaining guests at the tables to eat our turkey dinner.

We shared a table with a fair skinned, dark haired woman with brown eyes. Her name was Sarah and she had her two young children with her. Sarah appeared to be in her early thirties. Mikey was 6 years old and took on his mother's resemblance with straight, dark hair, while 3 year old Jeremy had curly blonde hair and light blue eyes. Both boys were equally adorable and could warm the hearts of anyone who spent more than a few minutes with them. Jeremy had quite an attachment to his dinosaurs that were all lined up next to his plate, while Mikey was a huge fan of hot wheels.

We learned that they were staying at the church's women's shelter after being displaced by their father, who ran out on the marriage with another woman. As a stay at home mother, Sarah couldn't afford the rent on her own until she could find a job that would allow for enough income to put Jeremy in daycare and cover the bills.

Across from us, on the other side of the table were a pair of homeless veterans. Bill and Eddie were quite the duo. I laughed so hard at all their jokes, my belly hurt. They had obviously formed a brotherly bond over the years. The pair had spent many years looking out for one another, on the streets. They both felt it was their solemn duty to protect the citizens of Boston.

I was halfway through my plate when Jasper excused himself from the table. A few minutes later, he returned a with 3 white envelopes. He handed Sarah, Bill and Eddie each their own envelopes and told them to open it up in private. I didn't get to see what was inside the envelopes, but I was sure he'd probably given them all the cash he'd had inside his wallet. They all thanked him before we left.

~

"This was such a sweet surprise!" I beamed, as I fastened my seat belt when we returned to Jasper's car to head home. "Thank you, Jasper. I truly had an amazing time with you, today."

"I'm so glad you enjoyed it. I always knew you might share this passion with me. It's why I love you so much." *Oh my God! Did he just say he loves me?*

"You have the biggest heart, Angel. I completely understand why you have a tendency to keep it concealed. It's meant to be protected. But I can clearly see the way your eyes light up when you are in service to others and how protective you are to the people you care about."

Hearing Jasper's words had me reeling so high, I could feel myself radiating from within. I did everything I could to fight back the tears, but I could still feel them, welling up inside my eyes. He truly did see me for all that I was.

"That's so sweet of you to say, Jasper." I said. "I love you, too! And I know you feel the same way about helping others. It's what I love the most about you." Jasper smiled. From the look in his eyes, I don't think he expected me to say I love you back, but I truly meant my words.

"I was thinking. Do you think you can take the week of Christmas off, at the coffee shop?" Jasper asked.

"It'll take some pretty persuasive swaying, for me to get Ben to agree, but I will see what I can do. We do have a new girl starting next week, maybe she can take my hours." I replied. "Why? What did you have in mind?"

"You'll see! Just do what you can do to get the time off." Jasper said as we turned into the parking garage.

When I told Jasper that Jamie was away visiting her folks in Virginia for the holiday, he offered to come and stay the night with me at Jamie's apartment, which was a first for us. He went upstairs to take Lucas out and joined me afterwards.

I couldn't wait to write all about my experience at the church with Jasper in my 'Never Forget' Journal. I caught him sneaking glances at me in between commercials while we were sprawled out on the couch, watching TV.

"What are you writing, Angel?" Jasper asked, curiously.

"I want to remember every detail of this day, so I'm writing it all down." I replied, shyly. "I keep a journal of my favorite memories, so I can always look back on them, whenever I want to."

"You do? That's adorable." Jasper smiled. "Do you have any memories of me in that thing?" He asked, with his famous smirk.

"Wouldn't you like to know?" I replied, teasingly.

"I would hope so, anyway." He replied.

"Well, I can tell you this… You're definitely in the one I'm writing now."

194

I said.

"I would never invade your private thoughts, Angel. I just think it's great that you have a creative outlet. Writing can actually be very therapeutic. Have you ever thought about writing about your other types of experiences? Like the ones you have with AJ? It might be a good way to release your pent up feelings." He said.

"You know, I never thought about doing that. Most of what I write about are happy memories." I replied.

"It can't hurt. It may be uncomfortable at first, but at least you can honor your feelings in some sort of way. It's kinda why I like to work out in the garden. One thing I always remembered about my mother, was her love of flowers. So when I put together all of those bouquets for the office, I feel connected to her in some sort of way and it always seems to brings me peace."

"I didn't know that. That's so sweet." I couldn't help but smile at his revelation. I had never met any guys who were into gardening before and always wondered what made it so special for him. "I suppose I could try, but I'll probably need to get a separate journal for that."

Jasper and I went to bed early since we both had to be up in the morning. We were both still so full from our Thanksgiving dinner, and far too tired to even think about christening my bed. It would have felt strange anyway, considering the bed wasn't technically mine, anyway. It belonged to Jamie's parents. Still it was nice, not having to spend the night alone on Thanksgiving, as I had initially had planned on. Having him with me made it a Thanksgiving I would never forget! Before I left for work the next day, we made plans for me to spend the night at his place the following night.

Chapter 36

I was stoked when I found out the bookstore was having a 25 percent off sale for Black Friday. I took some time on my break from the coffee shop to take advantage of the sale, browsing through the stationary aisle to find a new journal. I needed one I could write my darker thoughts and feelings in, like Jasper had suggested. I found a beautiful leather bound burgundy one I really liked. It looked very much like the one I got for my birthday, but this one had a fairly long leather drawstring that tied around it. It was a bit of a splurge at $29.99 for a journal, but with the ongoing sale and my added discount, I decided to take the plunge and went ahead and bought it for myself.

When I got back, Brooke and I exchanged our holiday stories from the previous day, in between customers.

"That's pretty amazing." She said, after I told her about the surprise outing Jasper had planned for our first Thanksgiving, together. "Sounds like you've really found yourself a keeper in Jasper!" She said, joyfully. Seeing her genuine smile let on to just how happy she was for me. Brooke really was a good friend.

"Our Thanksgiving turned out pretty well, too. It took a minute for Jason's parents to acclimate to my Mom and Grandma. They're both so expressive about their thoughts on everything." She laughed. "But boy did they love their cooking. Grandma made apple and pecan pies from scratch and my mom brought her famous deviled eggs. Jason's dad ate nearly half the tray of deviled eggs before dinner, and his mom went back for seconds on the pies. All in all, they seemed to get along pretty well together." She added with a smile.

"Aww. I love that for you." I said, smiling. "You and Jason really do make a great couple. Family is so important, it must be nice to know they all get along well with one another."

"I have to admit, I was a little nervous when we first got there, but it turned out better than I could have imagined." Brooke laughed at her recollection.

Brooke and I really banked on our tips that day. Our tip jar was so full, we had to make Ben empty it out and start a new one for us. We both had to stay a little later though, as we got a late rush in the afternoon. It seemed as though half of Boston was out and about shopping the stores for Black Friday. It was only natural that they would all pile in for their afternoon pick me up.

After work, I picked up a few more books to read from the sale, since I had more time to look around. Afterwards, I hurried home from work, excited to use my new journal. I lit my candle that Jasper bought me and sat down on the couch to write. I didn't quite know where to begin, so I wrote down anything that came to mind, in terms of my relationship with AJ. I had to admit, it was hard at first, facing those feelings again, but as it turned out, Jasper was right. It felt good to get it all out on paper. When I was finished, I had just enough time to take a short nap before heading into work at Silver Linings.

Chapter 37

O n my way to work, I felt a surge of freedom wash over me. The only way to describe how it felt was that my overall energy had become so light, it felt like I was one with the air around me. Like the darkness I had been harboring inside me for so long had suddenly vanished into thin air, leaving only the light behind. Only this light was so bright, it was too much to keep contained. I had to share this feeling. With someone. Anyone! *But who?* I wondered.

I started thinking about the girls who'd recently come to Silver Linings and everything they'd been through. They all seemed to be doing okay, but they just kind of stuck together most of the time, like a pack of wolves. I let myself wonder for a moment, as my thoughts stumbled across an epiphany. Maybe I could ask Maggie about having the girls do a writing exercise, like the one I did in my journal. Maybe it could help them release their pain, just as it did for me.

At first thought, I was afraid to overstep my boundaries. *I mean, who was I, but a mere receptionist?* I wasn't a counselor. I didn't have a college degree or anything. Deep inside, I knew my heart was in the right place, so I decided to follow where it was leading. The one thing I did have was my own experience, and how it helped me. Something inside me was telling me that I had to at least try! *What's the worst she could say? No?*

When I got to the office, I pitched my idea to Maggie, then offered to volunteer my time to come in on Saturday morning to share my experience with the girls and how it helped me.

"What a wonderful idea?" Maggie cried.

"Really? You think so?" I asked, still feeling a little self conscious.

"Absolutely. It certainly couldn't hurt!" She said, reassuringly. "You sure you're alright with giving up your Saturday morning, working two jobs?"

"Not at all." I replied. "Honestly, I really feel called to do this.."

"Well, that's very commendable. I knew there was a reason I liked you." Maggie smiled, before leaving me at my desk with my thoughts. I almost couldn't believe how welcome she was to my idea.

~

Later on that evening I came home to find Jasper in his penthouse, cooking something on the stove. I told him about my plans for Saturday morning. Like Maggie, he was also in full support of my taking the initiative to try and help the girls.

"I'm so glad it helped you feel better, Angel. I had a feeling it would." He smiled. "Maybe this can help them too." He said, carefully blowing the steam off of the spoon in his hand. He was giving me a taste of the kale and turkey sausage soup he was preparing us for dinner. "I'll be there tomorrow morning, too. We can go to lunch afterwards if you want."

"Mmm… This tastes incredible!" I said, handing him back the spoon. "Are you sure this is actually healthy?" I asked.

"Of course it is, it's loaded with veggies and Cannelloni beans for added protein. The diced tomatoes and Parmesan cheese are what gives it all the flavor. I made extra in case you want to take some home." He said.

"I'd like that. I'm sure Jamie will too." I said.

After dinner, Jasper suggested we walk Lucas over to the bookstore before it closed, so we could buy each of the girls their own journals to write in. He paid for them, of course, because it was far beyond my own budget to afford.

We stopped for ice cream on the way back. Jasper waited outside with Lucas while I went inside to place our order. An extra thick, chocolate malt for Jasper and a double scoop waffle cone filled with Rocky Road and Pistachio ice cream for myself. The girls behind the counter each took turns going outside to pet Lucas and were kind to give him his own special treat. A bowl of whipped cream sprinkled with mini dog treats. Lucas wolfed it down in less than 10 seconds, leaving behind a mustache of whipped cream on his scruff in the aftermath. The expression on Lucas's face was the best! The poor giant pup had no idea why I couldn't stop laughing and Jasper quickly joined in on the giggle fest.

When we got back to Jasper's penthouse, Jasper put Lucas in his crate for the night.

"I'm going to take a shower." Jasper said. My gaze was glued to his fingers as he teasingly unbuttoned the flannel shirt he was wearing. Jasper fixed his eyes on mine and I looked up to find that sexy smirk spreading across his face. "Care to join me?" He didn't wait for my answer and quickly began removing my shirt before I could even think about declining his request.

"Well, okay then." I laughed, nervously.

"Don't be shy with me now, Angel." He laughed as he went inside the bathroom to turn on the shower. "Come on."

Throwing caution to the wind, I stripped down to my bra and panties and followed him inside the bathroom. As the steam began to fill the air, the goddess inside me emerged. Arising from the space in my mind, confidently empowered by the magic of Jasper's loving gaze, as he watched my every move in wonder of what came next.

"You aren't going to shower in your underwear, are you?" He playfully teased.

"No." I said, as I boldly slipped off my bra. Jasper removed his boxer shorts in a show and tell, tit for tat. Soon we were both standing in the steam, face to face, completely bared to one another. Jasper stepped inside the shower first, and extended his hand to mine to join him.

"C'mon… The water is perfect." He said, as he stood behind me under the stream of the faucet. He smoothed his hands up my arms at each side, stopping to smooth his palm at the nape of my neck before slowly lifting my hair so he could pull it off to the side. He began trailing feather soft kisses up the side of my neck to the sensitive spot behind my ear until I could no longer contain the passion I had, building up inside me. I quickly turned my head and found his lips with my own. The water cascading above us felt warm and wet against my skin and the steam around us only fueled the passion in our kiss.

I turned around to face Jasper. He gently nudged me into a seated position on the bench and kissed his way down to my breasts, teasing my nipple with his teeth before plunging his full mouth over it. Sucking and teasing as if it were to produce honey, while feathering his fingers down my belly, working his way down to my clit, where he slowly began to massage in circular motions. I cried out in response, pleading for more. "Jasper, please."

He worked his middle finger in and out of me while rolling my clit between the pad of his thumb and his pointer finger as he sat down at the base of the shower. He pulled my ass forward so that he could get a better angle before diving into me with his mouth, sucking until I moaned. He was making a full course meal out of me as if he just couldn't get enough. "You taste so sweet, Angel" He said, as he continued sucking on my clit in full force, gliding his fingers in and out of me, slowly introducing his thumb to my rear for triple penetration.

"Eyes on me, Angel." He said. I opened my eyes and peered into his oceanic blue eyes. My orgasm came shortly after. I swear, he licked every bit of juice that fell out of me as if it contained the fountain of his youth. As the water crashed over me, my breaths soon began to steady and I could feel my heart rate slowly returning to normal.

Jasper stood me up inside the shower and bent me over the bench, where he slowly entered me with his full blown erection, sliding himself in and out of me like a pendulum. The intensity of his rhythmic pounding, over and over, soon had me come undone once more, in union with him.

"You're so fucking beautiful, Angel. How did I ever get so lucky?" He asked, as he began lathering me up with soap, before carefully washing my body from head to toe.

"I should say the same for you." I smiled, as I tousled my fingers through his wet hair, before we each climbed out of the stall. Having had two orgasms in less than 15 minutes, I was completely spent and we were both ready for bed.

Chapter 38

The next morning, I woke to the aroma of a steamy mug of coffee that Jasper had placed beside me on the nightstand. "I won't be gone long." He said as he pulled a crisp, white tee shirt over his head. The light of the sun speckled through his icy blue gaze when he kissed the top of my forehead. My waking moments were met with his warmest smile. That dimple of his had such a magical place inside my heart.

I sat up and sipped on my coffee, staring blankly, while Jasper finished getting dressed to take Lucas out for his morning walk. As my thoughts meandered toward the day I had ahead of me, I couldn't shake the feeling of nervousness. I was afraid of how the girls might take to my idea of helping them. Attempting to shake the unwelcome thoughts from my head, I quickly got out of bed and went inside the bathroom to splash some cold water on my face. I brushed my teeth and got dressed.

With a heavy need to distract my thoughts, before I wound up talking myself out of my plan, I went downstairs and roamed the pantry for something to cook us something light for breakfast. By the time Jasper and Lucas returned, our breakfast of scrambled eggs, toast and orange juice was ready and set out on the breakfast bar.

"It sure smells good in here." Jasper said as he joined me at the kitchen island. "What's cooking?"

"Nothing special, just breakfast." I said with a sigh.

Quickly sensing my unease, Jasper wrapped his arms around me from behind. "What's the matter, Angel?" He asked.

I drew in a quick breath before replying. "It's nothing, really." I said, nervously forking at my eggs as I turned my head to the side to face him. "I just hope that I'm not making a mistake, butting in on the girls and their recovery." Jasper released me from his embrace.

"Listen, Angel. You should never have to question anything you decide to do out of love. You can't hurt them any more than they've been hurt already." He said, urging me to look into his soulful, sapphire eyes. "Worst case scenario, they choose not to participate. Best case scenario, you hand them a key to something that just might truly help them. Anywhere in between can only be an improvement from where they are now, I promise you."

"You really think so?" I asked.

"I don't think so, I know so." He reiterated. "You got this! And remember... I won't be very far, if you need me."

~

When we arrived at Silver Linings, Jasper went to work out in the garden. I took the brown bag we brought from the book store, containing the journals and pens we bought and went in search of the girls. I found them all at the community table. They were finishing up their breakfast.

"I didn't know you work on Saturday." Lena said, as she turned to me in surprise. She had the friendliest demeanor I had seen her wear, yet. *OK! Maybe I can do this!* I thought to myself as Jasper's words of encouragement echoed though my mind.

"Well, technically, I don't usually work on Saturdays. I'm here on voluntary time today." I nervously stumbled out my reply. Attempting to steady my breath, I inhaled sharply before continuing.

"Listen." I said. "I have something for you all, but can you all please come outside with me for a few minutes?" The girls all looked confused, but they were all curious of what was in the bag I was holding, and quickly adhered to my request.

As we approached the soft grassy area of the garden, I let my eyes search out through the yard to find Jasper. He had already gone to work, raking up the fall colored leaves that had fallen to the ground. The air had that autumn crispness to it. The kind you wished you could bottle up and take out whenever you wanted to remember that feeling of warm fuzzy socks, pumpkin spice and everything nice. It was the kind of day you wished for when settling in to read a great book, with some warm tea or hot cocoa.

When we reached the desired spot I had chosen to do our writing exercise in, I turned to face the girls who were all now staring at me, waiting to hear what I had to say to them.

"What's in the bag?" One of the girls blurted out.

"You'll see in a minute." I replied, anxiously letting my nerves get the best of me. "Can we all just sit down and get comfortable?" I asked, taking the lead as I plopped my rear onto the greenery beneath our feet and sat in Indian style. Some of the girls were reluctant, but eventually joined me on the ground. "You all probably don't know this" I started to say, shakily as I worked myself in overtime trying to steady my breath. "I recently left a relationship where I was abused." They all just stared at me.

"Here," I said, as I reached inside the bag to hand them each their journals. "I brought you all here because I wanted to share something with you that really helped me."

"The pages are all blank." One of the girls laughed, as she ruffled through the pages.

"Yes." I said, as I reached into the bag to retrieve the pens. I passed them around to the girls. "These are journals. I brought them for you so you all can try to begin processing all of your thoughts about what you've all been through. The point is for you to release your feelings by writing them down." I said.

'So what? We're just supposed to sit here, writing?" The same girl asked.

"Yes. That's the plan, anyway." I laughed.

"Okay. I guess it won't hurt to give it a try." Another one of the girls said. *Thank God! Now if everyone will follow suit, we might actually get somewhere.*

We sat there in silence. It appeared they'd all gone along with the plan, until a few minutes later when I heard one of them huff out in frustration. "This is stupid! I'm not a writer!" She cried.

"Me either." Lena said, agreeing with the unruly girl. I looked over at Jasper who was lingering nearby within earshot of our conversation. He raised an eyebrow at me before silently calling me over, with his finger.

"Wait here a minute." I said as I stood up and walked over to where Jasper was working.

"This isn't working." I said, sighing.

"It *is* working, some of them are actually writing. Look!" He said, pointing in the direction of the girls who continued to write while I was gone. It was then that it hit me. Writing was my own creative outlet. Perhaps the girls who weren't writers might enjoy drawing or painting, or something else.

"Hmm… I have an idea! Thanks, Jasper." I said. I left him with a kiss on the cheek and hurried off, back to the girls.

"Okay. For those of you who don't write, try drawing instead for now." I said. "If that helps, I'll make sure we have something better for you next Saturday."

The rest of my time with the girls seemed to go a lot smoother. As it turned out, the opposing girls were actually pretty good at drawing. Lena drew a portrait of herself and her little sister, Alex that looked so life-like, we were all impressed. The other girl drew an amazing replica of the treeline behind the garden, where we were all sitting.

When we finished, I asked the girls to write down every ugly feeling they wanted to release onto a separate sheet of paper so we could do a burning ritual the following Saturday. It took me by surprise, but everyone agreed.

~

Chapter 39

L ater on that day, when Jasper and I went to lunch, I was so
excited about how everything turned out with the girls. I just
had to call Jamie and tell her the news.

"That's really great!" Jamie cried over the speaker phone. With Jasper
sitting next to me, I didn't want to be rude."I knew you'd find a way
to shine your light at Silver Linings. All you needed was to get your
foot in the door. Have you thought about taking it a step further and
enrolling in college?"

"Oh, I don't know about that, I'm already working two jobs, and I
definitely can't afford tuition." I replied.

"I'm sure they have scholarships and grants you can look into." Jamie
suggested. "It's definitely worth a shot."

"She wouldn't need a scholarship," Jasper was quick to interject. "If
you want to go to school, Angel, you know I got you. I think it's a great
idea. I was actually going to bring that up to you, myself." He said as

he forked his way into his Chicken Caesar Salad. Jasper's salad looked really good. I silently wished I had gone with that option instead of the meatloaf sitting on the plate in front of me. I ordered it from the special.

"You already do so much for me, you don't have to pay for my schooling too." I laughed.

"It's no burden, I can promise you that, but if you want to look into the scholarships, by all means. Just don't let it stand in the way of you making that decision. We'll work it out, regardless." Jasper said.

"I agree." Jamie said through the line. I was so surprised by Jasper's offer, I nearly forgot that Jamie was on the phone. "Think of it as an investment in your future, you should totally take his offer. Who knows, maybe you can intern at your job."

"You know what," I said into the phone, so they could both hear me, "maybe I will look into it."

"Listen Jamie, I've been meaning to ask you about something, do you have a minute to talk?" Jasper asked into the phone.

"Sure." Jamie replied. "What's up?" she asked.

Jasper wiped the corner of his mouth with his napkin and stood up from the table, while gesturing me to hand him my phone. "Finish your lunch, Angel. This won't take long." He said before walking outside to talk to Jamie in private. *Where was he going? And what's with all the secrecy?* I wondered. I watched him walk outside through the window of the booth where we were sitting. He was pacing back and forth on the sidewalk. I don't know what he was talking to her about, but he sure had plenty to say. Whatever they spoke about had him looking like the cat that ate the canary, when he returned shortly after.

"What was that all about?" I asked. I was dying to know.

"Oh, nothing." He said, grinning as he handed me back my phone.

"Hello?" I said into the phone.

"She hung up. She said to tell you she'll see you on Monday when she gets back."

"So you're really not going to tell me?" I laughed.

"You'll find out, Angel. In due time." He said with a smile. "Are you gonna finish that or do you want a box to take it home?" Jasper asked, pointing to my plate.

"Not unless we can feed it to Lucas." I giggled.

"Well, I'm sure he'd like that, but it's probably not the best idea." He chuckled."You barely ate. Do you want the rest of my salad? It's really good." *I thought he'd never ask!*

"Only if you're not gonna finish it." I replied. Jasper slid his plate over to my side of the table. It was so good, I finished every bit of what was left.

~

Later that evening, when I stepped out of the shower, I heard Jasper talking on the phone with someone, but I couldn't make out who it was. After a minute of eavesdropping, I felt a wave of guilt blow over me for listening in on him through the bathroom door. When I emerged from the bathroom, Jasper was sitting on his bed. I stood at the foot of his bed in only a towel with my hair wrapped up on top of my head. He looked up at me and smiled.

"Okay, I'll tell him." Jasper said to whoever he was talking to on the phone, "Yes, I'll let you know what happens, I gotta go. I'll talk to you tomorrow." Jasper said as he hung up from the call that he was on.

Before I could even ask, Jasper answered the question I had written on my face. "That was Sam."

"Oh, yeah?" I asked. I was more curious now, then ever. No one had heard a peep from him since he'd left for New York to go pay off his debt.

"He wants me to have Dimitri meet him in New York. Apparently they found Alex." Jasper said.

"I see." Having no idea who *Alex* was, I flashed him another puzzled look. "Who's Alex?" I asked.

"From what I understand, Alex is the reason why Lena was after my money in the first place." Jasper said. I just stared blankly, urging him to continue. "Remember how I told you how Sam met Lena?"

"Yes. You said she was a prostitute, working for the mob, like the other girls at Silver Linings."

"Right, well apparently, Alex is Dimitri and Lena's younger sister." Jasper paused to consider a thought he wasn't speaking. "You know... you might want to sit down for this, because it really is sick." Jasper said in forewarning.

"Okay." I said, "Let me go get dressed." I pulled my pajamas out of my overnight bag and went inside the bathroom to change. When I came back out, I took a seat on the other side of Jasper's bed.

"So as you know, Lena and Dimitri were both trafficked into the states. Lena was a prostitute, yes, but before these girls become of age to roam the streets for these sick bastards, they're handed off to a different sort of clientele." Jasper cleared his throat and searched my eyes to gauge my reaction. "The kind that pay big money to get their jollies off on underage girls." I felt my stomach twist at Jasper's revelation.

"Oh my God. How awful? Do you mean to tell me that Lena ..." I couldn't bring myself to even speak the words. *No wonder why she was so fucked up!*

"Yes." Jasper said, relieving me of saying the words. "So, Sam has no way of getting in touch with Dimitri or Lena. He needs one of them to come to New York to take custody of Alex."

"That makes sense. I can see why Sam doesn't want Lena to come, it's too dangerous." I said, crawling into Jasper's arms for comfort. My heart hurt so badly for the girls at Silver Linings. I could only imagine the things they must have gone through.

"I know this is a lot, Angel." Jasper said, smoothing his thumb over the side of my face to console me. "I didn't want to keep you in the dark about what's going on."

"I appreciate that." I said. Even though the reality of the situation hit me pretty hard, I was grateful for Jasper's honesty.

Chapter 40

When Jamie returned from her trip on Monday evening, I told her about everything that transpired while she was gone. She was just as shocked as I was about the girls.

"Wow. There's some really sick people in this world. I actually feel bad for Lena, now. Can you imagine knowing that your sister was still out there having to go through it all?" She asked.

"Yes…. I can imagine and I can barely handle doing that!" I replied, shaking my head. "How did your weekend go with your folks?" I asked, trying to change the subject.

"It was fun. My parents send their regards." Jamie said as she wheeled her suitcase across the living room floor to her bedroom door. "I ate so much, I had to change out of my jeans and into my fat pants. " Jamie laughed. "It was nice. How about you? How did your weekend go with Jasper?"

I told her about how Jasper and I spent our Thanksgiving, serving the homeless at the church.

"You guys are like two peas in a pod, you know. I swear, that man was born to be with you." She beamed. "I'm so glad you decided to come to Boston. You two would never have met, if you hadn't."

"That's true." I agreed. "Speaking of Jasper, what were you two talking about on the phone the other day?" I asked, hoping she might throw me a bone.

"Oh, nothing." She teased.

"Come on, Jamie. You have to tell me something. It's in our BFF code of ethics." I laughed.

"He just wanted some insight on what to get you for Christmas." She said, clearly hoping I would take the bait.

"I don't believe you. You guys were talking for a good 10 minutes." I said.

"Nope, that was all." Her eyes were smiling at me. "And, no, I'm not telling you what he's getting you either, so don't even ask! Besides, you love surprises, and trust me when I tell you, you're gonna love this one. Besides, what kind of BFF would I even be if I gave it up and spoiled the surprise?"

"Alright, alright. I guess I'll just have to wait another two weeks to find out." I said, flashing her my best puppy dog eyes.

"Good. You'll be happy you waited, I promise!" She said. Clearly, she wasn't budging, but I had to at least try.

We ordered Chinese take out for dinner and watched movies while catching up about our holidays. I told Jamie about the people we met at our table at the church and what Jasper did for them before we left. Neither of us could imagine what it would've been like to have children and find out that our husband was cheating.

"I would take my kids and run." Jamie said. While I wondered if that would be something I was strong enough to do on my own.

"You would?" I asked. "Even if you had nowhere to go and had to stay in a shelter?"

"Hell yeah! Why would I let my children stay around a piece of shit like that?" Jamie seemed pretty solid on her statement. "Especially boys. I wouldn't want to take my chances on them growing up to think that it was okay to treat women that way."

"I guess you're right." I said, taking on her perspective. "Well, I think I better turn in. I have work in the morning."

"Maybe I should too. It's been a long day, I am pretty tired." Jamie agreed as she turned off the TV. We both stood up from the couch and went to bed.

I sent Jasper a text message to say good night. After spending the weekend at his penthouse, it felt strange going to bed without him. Jasper quickly chimed back.

Jasper:

Good night, Angel. Wish you were here.

Me:

Me too. I'll see you tomorrow. Xo

I remembered to say a prayer for all the girls, the woman and her kids and the pair of veterans we met at the church, as I lay in bed that night. I fell asleep remembering the words Jasper had once said to me. "Bad things happen to good people and we have no control over them, but we can always learn and grow from them." It made me realize just how much I had grown since I had made the decision to leave AJ. It was my hope for all the girls that they would, someday too.

Chapter 41

Christmas Eve 2012

"The car is packed and Lucas is at his new Doggy Daycare. Are you ready to go?" Jasper asked when he came to pick me up for our trip.

"As ready as I can be, since I don't know where we're going." I had to laugh at just how many times I'd been in this position, ever since I'd met Jasper. Jasper took hold of the handle on my suitcase Jamie had let me borrow. It was stuffed to the brim. We were only going to be gone for a few days, but I packed enough clothes for the week, just in case of anything.

"I'm just glad you were able to get the time off." Jasper said to me as I followed him out to the elevator. I felt so bad, leaving Jamie behind to spend Christmas alone here, without me, but I was equally excited to see where Jasper was taking me. I felt a little better when Jamie told me she had plans to spend Christmas with Dillon.

"Give me a minute." Jasper said, as we stepped out of the elevator. I watched him walk over to the security desk, where he reached into the breast pocket of his winter coat to produce an envelope to give to Charlie.

"Merry Christmas, Charlie. This is for you. Thank you for your service." Jasper said with a smile that could light up the world.

"Oh, thank you very much, Mr. Sullivan!" Charlie said in surprise, as I watched the smile climb across his face. "It's my pleasure! Merry Christmas to you too!"

"Merry Christmas, Charlie!" I called out, as I waved to him from where I stood by the door to the parking garage.

"Merry Christmas, Miss Taylor!" Charlie chimed back. "Hope you two have fun!"

"Oh we definitely will!" Jasper called back as he walked out into the garage and held the door open for me to follow him, outside. It was so cold outside, I had to rearrange my scarf to shield myself from the draft. Jasper quickly opened the passenger door for me, before walking around his SUV to load my suitcase into the trunk.

"You're really not gonna tell me where we're going?" I asked when he got behind the wheel.

"What fun would that be?" Jasper laughed. "I'm sure you'll figure it out along the way."

Jasper packed us a cooler full of car snacks to nibble on for our drive.

We took turns, playing DJ. I sang along to nearly every song that came on the radio. Jasper even sang with me on a few of the songs that he knew. Suddenly, it dawned on me that our destination no longer mattered to me. I was already having the time of my life on our journey to get there.

At some point, I must have fallen asleep on the drive. When I opened my eyes, I glanced at the clock on the dash to see that it was 2:14 pm. I gathered my surroundings, seeking clues to where we were. I had my answer in an instant when the Statue of Liberty came into view, across the water.

"Wait, are we spending Christmas in New York?" I asked, excitedly as I rubbed the sleep from out of my eyes. *Please let it be New York City!* I wished in silence. *Please, please, please!*

"Ding Ding Ding Ding Ding! Tell her what she's won!" Jasper replied in a teasing manner.

"Oh my God. Are you serious?! This is perfect!" I cried. "Did I ever tell you I was actually born in New York?" I asked.

"Yes, you did, actually. I think it was on our first date." He replied.

"I haven't been here since I was a kid." I cried, as happy tears began to well inside my eyes.

After finally making it through New York City traffic in one piece, Jasper pulled into the valet station at the Waldorf Astoria. "We're here." Jasper said.

We were greeted by a silver haired man with a full beard and mustache, wearing a navy blue uniform and white gloves. His cheeks were rosy red from the cold when he flashed me a smile, before opening my car door. He reached inside the car for my hand to help me out of the passenger side of Jasper's SUV and I waited outside in the frosty air for Jasper to hand him his keys. The sky was overcast. It was cold enough to snow, but the ground was still dry.

After the bellhop took our bags from the trunk, he loaded them onto a dolly cart and handed Jasper a white ticket to give to the bellhop desk. Jasper soon joined me where I stood by the door, waiting to go inside. We were both happy to step in from the cold, where it was warm. My eyes lit up when we stepped inside the grand entrance of the hotel. There were floor to ceiling windows, each aligned with beautifully decorated Christmas trees, taller than any I had ever seen before.

Jasper took my hand and guided me toward the bellhop desk, where he handed the ticket for our bags to the attendant. From there, we were directed across the beige, marble floors with a large navy blue and circular design in the center, to a row of mahogany desks, where we could check into the hotel.

"You're all set to check in." Said the middle aged, brunette woman behind the check in desk. She handed Jasper the keys to our room.

"Thank you. Can you please point me in the direction of the concierge?" Jasper asked.

"Of course, sir." The woman replied, as she pointed to her neighboring co-worker. "Eric will be glad to help you with anything you need."

"Perfect. Thank you." Jasper said to the woman. "Wait here a minute, Angel. I'll be right back."

"Okay." I said, as I stood there, awkwardly staring at the woman. I wondered what Jasper was up to, now. The woman just smiled in return. A moment later, Jasper returned.

"Okay! Let's go!" Jasper said as he took my hand. To my surprise, he led me back in the direction of the same door we came in at.

"Wait! Aren't we going up to our room?" I asked.

Jasper flashed me a mischievous grin, "Nope. There's plenty of time for that later." He said. "We have plans!"

"We do?" I asked, trying to keep up with his pace as we made our way out of the hotel lobby and back out onto the street.

"Yes!" Jasper said.

"But it's so cold outside." I whined.

"Don't worry, Angel. I'll keep you warm, I promise." Jasper said, pulling me closer to his chest. We walked over to an overhead area that looked like a bus stop, where there were several people sitting on a bench waiting. Before I knew it, we were all lined up to load the trolley that had the words Rockefeller Center flashing across the screen. I had never been there before, but it was common knowledge on what it was known for.

"Are we going to see the big tree?" I asked, excitedly.

"You'll see." Jasper smiled. When the trolley came to a stop, everyone stood to exit the vehicle. Jasper gave the driver a tip and stepped down, before reaching for my hand to help me down the steps.

We lingered back a bit to let the crowd from the trolley out ahead of us and Jasper and I walked hand in hand as we approached the enormous Christmas tree. My eyes lit up as they danced across to find the giant rink where many people were found, skating across the ice.

"Have you ever been ice skating before?" Jasper asked me as we approached the stand, where we could rent our skates.

"Roller skating was my favorite thing to do as a teenager. I've only been ice skating once, on a school field trip when I was 10." I laughed.

"It's like roller skating, but a little different." Jasper said.

The rental attendant handed us our skates. We found a bench to sit down and put them on, before heading out onto the ice. I held onto Jasper for dear life, praying I wouldn't lose my balance and fall. Jasper took me over to the edge where I could hold on to the wall, while he demonstrated what to do. I was honestly shocked at how skillful he was on the ice. "It's not hard... just like roller skating, only you have to bend your knees slightly." He called out as he skated out to the center of the rink and returned back to where I remained, stagnantly hugging the wall.

"Easier said than done!" I giggled.

"You got this," Jasper said. "Here, take my hand!" He said. I let go of the wall to reach for Jasper's hand. He coaxed me around the rink, while I held on to the wall. Once we completed the circle, Jasper thought it was a good idea to graduate to the center of the rink.

"You can do it, I'm right here." Jasper said. I slowly put my faith into his words and got out of my own head. Tuning into the Christmas music that filled my ears, I let go of the wall to join him. He skated in front of me, holding both of my hands. "You see, I won't let you fall, Angel, I promise." Just as fast the words fled from his mouth, a pair of skaters flew past us both, sweeping me off my balance. I fell onto the ice with a thud, dragging Jasper down with me because he never let go. We both rolled over laughing hysterically.

"Okay, I take it back! I won't let you fall, alone." Jasper laughed. He quickly swept me into his arms to shield me from a group of skillful skaters, who quickly passed us by. He held me for a moment as we both lay on the floor of the rink.

"You okay?" He asked.

"I'm fine." I replied, sitting up to brush the icicles off my winter coat. We both looked up into the clouds as the snow began to fall from the sky.

"Okay. I think we've had enough for now." Jasper laughed as he rose to his feet. He reached down to help me up, off the ice. "Let's go get some hot cocoa."

I was grateful for the experience, but equally as happy to get my skates off and slip back into my boots. We turned in our skates and headed over to the refreshment counter to get some hot cocoa. While we were waiting in line, I felt someone tap me on the shoulder from behind. I couldn't believe my eyes when I turned around to see Jamie with a big fat grin on her face.

"Oh my God! What are you doing here?" I cried.

"Surprise!" She shouted, as she embraced me in a giant hug.

"I thought you and Dillon were spending Christmas together in Boston." Clearly I thought wrong. I caught sight of Dillon watching us from behind with a goofy looking grin on his face. Jasper walked over to him and gave a slap shake to his hand.

"Wait... there's someone I want you to meet." Jamie said as she called out to an adorable little girl with dark brown banana curl pigtails peeking out from her bright red ear muffs. She was standing off to the side, next to a woman with dark hair and fair skin who appeared to be a few years older than Jamie and me. "Emily, come over here and meet my best friend." The little girl let go of her mother's hand and ran over to where we stood.

As she approached, she stretched her bright pink glove out to shake my hand. "Hi. I'm Emily." She said with a rosy cheek, smile so big, it revealed her missing two front teeth.

"Hi Emily, my name is Carla. It's so nice to meet you! I've heard so many wonderful things!" I said in exchange of her greeting.

Dillon introduced Jasper and me to Theresa, Emily's mother, and we all found a cozy spot to sit down and enjoy each other's company. It didn't take long before Jasper invited both Theresa and Emily to join us for dinner that night. Apparently, this was his and Jamie's secret plan all along.

"I appreciate the invitation," Theresa said, before politely declining Jasper's offer. "I have plans to meet my fiance's family tonight for Christmas Eve dinner.

"I'll come! Can I go, Mom? Please?" Emily joyfully pleaded with her mother.

"Of course you're coming, sweetheart, you're with us!" Dillon said, playfully to Emily.

"Yay!" She cried out.

"Well, we better get going. We have something to tend to before dinner." Jamie said, with a smile in Jasper's direction that left me wondering what she was up to. "We'll see you guys later." Jamie said, as she stood up from the table.

"Wow, it is getting late!" Theresa said, after glancing at her watch. "I should get going too! Wesley is picking me up in an hour." She gave Emily a squeeze, and excused herself from the table. "I hope you have fun tonight, Ems."

"Thanks Mom. You too! Tell Wesley I said hi!" Emily said to her mom before she too, stood up from the table. She took Jamie and Dillon's hands and sandwiched herself in between them. I couldn't help but smile at how happy they all appeared to be, together.

"Well, seeing as though we're the only ones left, maybe we should start heading back to the hotel." Jasper said to me.

"Sounds good to me." I agreed with a yawn. I was growing tired from all of the excitement. "I sure wouldn't mind fitting in a nap, before we go to dinner."

"Sounds like a plan." Jasper agreed.

Chapter 42

L ater that evening, Jasper and I were the first ones to arrive at the restaurant. The festive sound of holiday music danced through the halls that were decked in the finest of holiday decor. Jasper and I took our seats at a table that was beautifully set for eight. I had just assumed we wouldn't fill all the seats, but when Jamie, Dillon and Emily appeared with the host, I screamed out in joy at who came trailing in behind them.

"Mama!" I shouted! "Abby... Oh my God! You guys are here!" I was beginning to tear up, I was so happy to see them. I watched the biggest smile curve across Jamie's face at my reaction. I quickly rose to my feet to hug them all.

"Hi Baby. Merry Christmas!" Mama said as she leaned into my embrace.

"Come here, Abby." I said, pulling her in for a hug, too. She looked so beautiful, standing there in her crimson, red gown. Seeing Abby in a dress was always a rare occasion, it honestly took my breath away.

"Merry Christmas." Abby said. She was also happy to see how surprised I was.

"Merry Christmas." I replied. "Oh my God, I'm so glad you guys are here."

With all the excitement, I barely noticed the tall and slender, salt and pepper haired man that was standing there with them.

"Carla, this is Bill. He's my… friend." Mama said with a sheepish grin. *WHAT?!*

I was stunned. *Pull yourself together!* I quickly told myself, as I extended my hand out to greet him, hello. "Hi, I'm Carla." I said.

"Pleasure to meet you, Carla." He said, as everyone began to take their seats.

"How about a Shirley Temple for the little one, eh?" The waiter asked as he began to fill everyone's glasses with the bottle of champagne Jasper had ordered for the table. "I'll be right back, madame." He said, flashing Emily a big smile.

"Oh my God, did you really plan all of this for me?" I asked, smothering Jasper with kisses before I sat down at the table, next to him. Jasper's smile stretched from ear to ear. "This was such a great surprise!"

"Anything for my beautiful Angel, but if I'm truly being honest, I brought them all here for a bit of a selfish reason." Jasper said to me before turning to everyone at the table.

"Thank you all for coming. As you probably know, Carla is a very special person to me. It doesn't take a rocket scientist to figure out that she's the reason I've felt so alive from the moment I first laid eyes on her." Jasper paused to reflect on his thoughts. "It's no secret, we've been through many ups and downs these past few months, but I have come to a realization that there is absolutely no one else that I would rather ride this storm with, than her. She is passionate, caring and incredibly strong. Watching her grow through everything she has been through has been an incredibly, inspiring experience I will forever be grateful for." Jasper cleared his throat, as if he was nervous, while I had turned three shades of beet red from all of the attention I had been given with his words."And so…. With all of your blessings, it would make me the happiest man alive to ask for her hand in marriage." My jaw dropped when he lowered himself down to one knee, at my lap. "That is, of course, if she is willing to have me." He laughed, nervously, before reaching into the breast pocket of his brown, leather jacket to retrieve a navy blue velvet box. "What do you say, Angel?" He asked. His hands were visibly shaking when he opened the box to reveal a stunning, princess cut diamond set in a beautiful, white gold infinity band. All the women at the table gasped."Will you marry me, Angel?"

I was speechless and breathless all at once. I looked deep into the pool of his ocean blue eyes, while Jasper and everyone else at the table eagerly awaited my response. I reminded myself to breathe as I glanced around the table at all the people I cared about the most, nodding their heads in support of my reply. I could only say what any girl in their right mind would say to the man of her dreams, kneeling before her.

"Yes…. A million times, YES!" I cried. "Jasper Sullivan, I would be honored to be your wife." A round of applause echoed throughout the entire restaurant. Mama, Jamie and I were all in tears.

"That's great, because I have so many dreams for the future, and there isn't a single one without you in it, Angel." Jasper said. *Omg!* I was still blushing, as I wiped the tears away from my eyes. Jasper quickly came to my rescue from embarrassment when he pulled me in for a kiss to seal the deal.

"Can I be the flower girl?!" Emily shouted! "Mommy says I get to be *her* flower girl, so I'll already have a dress!" We all laughed at her joyful eagerness to join in on the celebration.

"With an adorable face like yours, how can I guy say no?" Jasper replied to Emily. "But as with any marriage, I will need to consult with my soon to be wife. What do you think, Angel? Can Emily be our flower girl? Pretty please?" Jasper asked with his best puppy dog eyes.

"Of course you can be our flower girl." I said with a smile in Emily's direction. After a few minutes of congratulatory conversation, I stood up from the table and walked over to where Mama was sitting. I was dying to know more about this mysterious guy, named Bill, she'd brought as her date. I also wanted to see how she truly felt about everything. "Can I talk to you for a minute, in private?" I asked with a whisper to her ear. Mama stood up from the table to excuse herself.

"Looks like I have some explaining to do." She said flashing her famous southern smile at everyone. "We'll be back in a bit."

Mama followed me over to the restroom where I began to drill her about Bill.

"So…. Who's this guy you brought with you? And how come I haven't heard anything about him?" I asked.

"It's a funny story, actually," Mama said, as she nervously fiddled with her satin, green gown in the mirror. I couldn't get over how good she looked. Her shoulder length, auburn hair was curled, and her skin was glowing. Whoever this man was, I was sure he had something to do with her looking ten years younger. "One your sister should probably tell you," Mama laughed to herself, "Abby was tired of watching me sit at home, alone every night while she was hanging out with her friends. She and her friends came up with this grand scheme to set up a dating profile for me on Plentyoffish.com.

"You're kidding!" I said. "And you agreed to do it?" I asked.

"I didn't have much of a choice in the matter, she did it without me knowing." Mama laughed. I laughed too because I could totally see Abby doing that.

"So how did you wind up dating if you didn't even know about the profile?" I asked, curiously.

"Abby orchestrated the whole thing. She set me up on a blind date with him. He met us at the bowling alley and rented the lane beside us." Mama laughed as she recalled the memory. "Afterwards, he asked me for my number. I thought he seemed nice enough to be friends with, so I gave it to him. That was only after giving him my sob story about not being over Joel, of course. A few days later, Joel came to visit me in a dream. He said he wants me to be happy. I didn't understand it at first, but when Bill called me a few days later to ask for a date, something told me to give him a chance. I'm so glad I did, honey. He is the sweetest man. Joel would have loved him."

"I'm so happy for you, Mama. You've worked so hard, all your life, you deserve to be happy." I said, as I reached over to give her a hug.

"Thank you, Baby. That means a lot. Honestly, I'm pretty sure I have you to thank for it." She said, wiping the tears away from her eyes.

"You do?" I asked, wondering what she meant.

"Yes, when you came back home and helped me sort through everything in my apartment, it stirred up some feelings I had been suppressing for a while. It felt good to let it go. I don't think I would have even considered the idea of dating again if I still had all that stuff staring back at me all the time. It was time to let it go."

"Well, you know I'm always happy to help, Mama. You know that." I said.

"Of course, I know that, sweetie. I think we should probably get back to your fiance before he sends out a search and rescue party to come find us." Mama said.

"You're probably right." I agreed with a giggle.

Mama draped her arm around my shoulder and we both exited the bathroom. On our way back to the table, she halted me before we got to the table and said, "I am so happy for you, baby. Jasper's going to make such a wonderful husband... I can't believe my baby's getting married!"

"Thank you, Mama. I think I really lucked out this time." I said in response, before we both went back to our table to find our seats.

Chapter 43

After dinner, Dillon invited us all back to his house for coffee and dessert. Mama, Abby and Bill piled into the backseat of Jasper's SUV and we followed Dillon and Jamie to Dillon's house. When we pulled into Dillon's driveway, Jasper received a phone call from Sam, and told us all to go inside without him.

"I'm sorry, I have to take this. You guys go on ahead, I'll meet you all inside." Jasper said as we all got out of the car and followed the colorful string of lights as they led up to his front door. I was grateful I had chosen to wear my boots, as I felt the snow crunch beneath my feet.

Dillon held the door open for us as we entered the foyer to his home. We were all fascinated by his eye for detail as he took our coats while we lingered around admiring his ability to deck the halls. After hanging our coats in the closet, he led us across the hard wood floors, down the hallway to the living room where we all gathered by the tree to gawk. Dillon fiddled with the remote control on his TV to find a station that played Christmas music and I sat down to take my boots off the moment I realized the floors of the living room were draped in tan Berber carpet.

"I'll get the fire started. Please, make yourselves at home." Dillon gestured for us to sit down as he began to poke around at the logs inside the fireplace.

"I'll go make some coffee." Jamie offered, while Mama, Bill and I took our seats on Dillon's tan leather couch. Abby and Emily were still over by the tree, looking for the switch to turn on the train that tracked around the living room.

I was happy to have some time to get to know Bill a little more. I began drilling him with all sorts of questions about his family and what he did for a living. I learned quite a bit in the few minutes we had to chat. He was a great sport and seemed more than happy to settle my curiosity. I learned that he was a recently retired army veteran who served in the Vietnam war. He spoke highly of the four children he had of his own, which he mostly raised on his own after his wife left him for another man. His youngest was a few years younger than me. He was divorced for just over 12 years and had his first grandson on the way.

"So, what made you decide to start dating again?" I asked, curious as to why he waited so long.

"Well, with my grandson coming in February, I thought it would be nice to share these milestones with someone special. Now that I'm retired and all of my kids have flown the coop, I have far too much free time to spend all alone." His response made sense. He seemed kind enough and oddly reminded me a bit of Joel in his well mannered demeanor. All in all, he seemed like a great match for Mama. If she was happy, I was more than happy to learn that she decided to date again. I always thought she was far too young to live the rest of her life alone. Abby was getting older now too, and I knew she wouldn't live with Mama forever.

"Well, you sure picked a great catch." I said with a wink in Mama's direction.

Jamie brought the tray of coffee out into the living room and placed it on the coffee table so we could all prepare our cups as we desired. I couldn't help but wonder where Jasper was. He sure was taking a while on the phone with Sam. Just as I finished preparing his cup, I decided to put my boots back on to go find him. As soon as I grabbed my coat from the closet, I heard the door swing open. Jasper walked in with a great big smile splattered across his face.

"I just got the best news we could ever ask for." Jasper said to me as he walked through the door. I could tell by the smile on his face and the light in his eyes that whatever he had to tell me was gonna make me even happier than I already was.

"Sam and Dimitri are back in Boston. They're on their way over to the Christmas party at Silver Linings to surprise Lena with Alex. He didn't go over all the details with me, but apparently, the men who were trafficking the kids from Russia were all arrested in a giant sting operation. Many other kids, just like Alex, were rescued from the house where they were all being kept."

"Oh my God, are you serious? That's incredible!" I cried. *Could this night get any better?* I wondered.

"That's what he said, anyway. I'm sure we'll be hearing more about it when we get back." Jasper said as we made our way back to the living room to join everyone and take our seats. After telling everyone the story behind what happened, we shared the good news with them.

"That sure sounds like a Christmas miracle if I ever heard one." Bill said, joyfully. Everyone agreed.

"Well, it wouldn't be Christmas without gifts!" Dillon said as he began pulling the beautifully wrapped presents out from under the tree. I couldn't believe he had something for everyone, including Abby and Bill. Being the gift giver that I was, I was embarrassed that I didn't have a gift for anyone besides Jasper, and that was back at the hotel. I had planned on giving it to him on Christmas morning.

Being the youngest, Emily was the first to open her gift. Her eyes lit up when she opened up her first tablet. "You're the best, Daddy. Thank you, thank you, thank you!" She cried as she got up to wrap her arms around Dillon and plant him with kisses.

Abby was next in line. She smiled big when she discovered the pair of state of the art headphones when she opened her gift.. "These are great! Thank you!"

"I may have had some redirection on that one." Dillon winked at Jamie.
\

"His first pick was makeup." Jamie laughed because she knew well enough that Abby would never wear it, being the tomboy that she was.

Mama and Bill were both thankful for their gift card for dinner and a bottle of wine.

"This was so nice of you to consider us too, thank you." Mama said to Dillon.

I was next, and my gift had both mine and Jasper's name on it. "It's so pretty! Did you wrap all of these yourself?" I asked Dillon as I slowly tugged at the bow, stalling as I always did when it came to opening my own gifts.

"I may have had some help with that one." Dillon replied.

I opened the box, to find another smaller box inside. Each time I thought I got to the box with the gift inside, it was another box that opened to another smaller box. When I finally opened the smallest box, I damn near cried at what I saw. "Oh my GOD! Tickets to see Annie on Broadway?" I quickly jumped to my feet to give Jamie and Dillon a great big hug. "This is the best gift! Thank you!" I cried as I caught Mama smiling at my gift because she knew how many times I watched that movie over and over as a little girl.

"I feel bad, I don't have any gifts for anyone here." I said.

"Don't worry, Angel, I got you." Jasper said as he reached into his pocket and drew out an envelope. "Sorry, it isn't wrapped. Emily, will you do the honors?"

Emily quickly jumped up from the floor where she was sitting to be the first to see what the envelope contained. She pulled out the envelope's contents, revealing several tickets that looked oddly similar to the ones that were inside my gift. "Little Orphan Annie The Musical." She slowly read out loud to everyone.

243

"Hold on… Let me see that!" Jamie said, excitedly as she reached for the tickets in Emily's hands so she could see for herself. "Looks like we're all going to Broadway to see Annie!" Jamie shouted, excitedly.

"In all the years I lived in New York, I've never been to a Broadway show." Mama said with a clap of her hands.

"Well, this is the first time I've ever been to NY, so I've never been to one either!" Abby shouted. She would never admit it, but I knew she loved Annie almost as much as I did. We used to watch the movie and sing along to all the songs together when she was little.

"This is the best Christmas ever!" I said, softly to Jasper with tears in my eyes as I leaned in and gave him another kiss to say thank you.

After sharing what was probably the tastiest Christmas cookies I had ever had in my entire life, we made Dillon tell us where he bought them from so we could bring some home to Boston with us.

We all sat there in Dillon's living room singing Christmas carols by the fireplace until we ran out of songs to sing. The magic of Christmas was clearly in the room and we all felt it inside our hearts as we said our goodbyes for the night.

~

When we all piled into Jasper's SUV to head back to the hotel, Jasper had one more surprise up his sleeve for Mama and Abby. He reached across my lap to open the glove compartment box and pulled out a Christmas card to hand to Mama. "This is for you, Corrine." I had no idea he had something else planned for her.

244

"You're family now, son." She said with a proud smile as she took the envelope from his hand. "You can call me Mama." Mama did seem quite pleased with our engagement. "Should I open it now?" She asked.

"Whenever you want, just don't lose it." Jasper replied with a chuckle.

"Open it!" Abby cried out anxiously. "I wanna see!"

Mama gasped when she opened the card to find a check that was written out to her inside the card. "Thirty thousand dollars? I'm afraid I don't understand. What's this for?" She asked Jasper as I watched the tears begin to pool inside her eyes from the rear view mirror.

"That is for all the years you have spent working your tail off to raise your daughters. I have you to thank for my beautiful Angel, who I will soon have the privilege to call my wife." Jasper said, flashing a smile at me. "Please use it for a down payment on a house that you love. And if you ever need anything beyond that, don't hesitate to ask." Jasper replied as we pulled into the valet station of the hotel.

"I... I don't know what to say." Mama said with tears coming in full stream now. "Thank you, Jasper." Mama was clearly in shock, as were all the rest of us.

Even Bill choked up when he heard the news. "That's a generous gift." He said after clearing his throat.

"This really is the best Christmas ever!" Abby shouted as we all got out of Jasper's SUV.

I had to agree, there was no one more deserving than Mama to receive such a grand gift, but I had to wonder if maybe it was too much. "Are you sure about this Jasper? That's a lot of money for a gift." I asked him quietly when we got out of the car.

"It would make me happy to know that your mother is well taken care of. She deserves that and so much more for how well she did in raising you, Angel." He replied before Mama swooped in with a giant hug. "You have no idea how much this means to me." I heard her say to him as the snow began to fall from the sky.

"Look! It's snowing!" Abby cried, happily.

"It sure is… A Merry White Christmas." I said with a smile as we all began to make our way out of the frosty air and into the warm lobby of the hotel.

Chapter 44

Ϩ

Epilogue

We had a great time on our trip to New York. It was difficult to say goodbye to Mama and Abby, but we were all incredibly grateful to have spent the holiday together. When we got back to Boston, many of the girls, including Lena, came up to my desk over the next few weeks to thank me for helping them find a way to help them feel better. Maggie also gave praise to my work and told me she'd seen a big difference in the overall demeanor of the girls. They were all beginning to trust the other residents enough to participate in some of the community activities. She said they were like flowers in bloom as opposed to the 'trust no one' wolf pack, they'd all shown up in.

Mama wasted no time at all in finding her very own dream house, complete with a guest house in the back. It was a good thing that she and Bill hit it off, because she needed someone to help her with all the upkeep. After spending nearly every night with her for over six months, Bill finally decided to sell his own house and move in with her.

I eventually gave in to Jasper's offer of paying my tuition for college. Brooke and I both enrolled the following Fall semester. I majored in Psychology with an associates in English Literature. She and I shared a few writing classes together and I was incredibly grateful for my second chance at having a college experience, especially since I was able to share it with my new friend.

The following year, Jasper and I had a beautiful destination wedding in Greece. All of our closest family and friends were there to celebrate with us. Maggie opened up a special position just for me. I still helped with the switchboard, but my new title was creative counselor. After graduation, I became a writer of many successful books, including the story you are reading right now called the Silver Linings Trilogy. I couldn't believe that my first attempt at writing a story made the New York Times best sellers list! Offers for the movie rights came shortly after. After some careful consideration and the help of an agent, I found an offer I couldn't refuse.

Having my story on the big screen for millions of people to see has been one hell of a Silver Lining from where I first began in my journey of healing from my relationship with AJ. Life could not be better, or could it? On Jasper's 31st birthday, we found out that we would soon become the proud parents of our first baby, Sophia Ren'ee Sullivan, named after Jasper's mother and my grandmother.

~

Spring / 2019

Every year, we made our annual visit to Virginia for Spring break to see Mama, Bill and Abby. Mama refused to let us stay anywhere else but in her guest house so she could soak up all the time she had to spend with us. It became tradition for us to cook dinner for Mama and Bill on our last night of vacation. It was our way of saying thank you for taking Sophia out for the day, so Jasper and I could have a day of our vacation to ourselves before heading back home.

While Jasper and I were at the grocery mart, deciding which sauce to buy for our Chicken Parmesan dinner we had planned, I came across a familiar face. Though it was much slimmer than I had remembered, I knew that it was him. I would recognize those hazel green eyes anywhere.

"AJ? Is that you?" I asked. There was clearly no escape in running into him, he was in the same aisle of the store as we were. AJ looked up in surprise when he recognized who I was and placed the box of pasta he was holding inside his cart. "Carla…" he said, standing there awkwardly, trying to figure out what to say. "It's been a while. How are you?" He asked, cautiously as Jasper quickly drew his arm around my shoulder to ensure that I was safe. "Jasper, is it?" Jasper nodded in AJ's direction. We had learned of AJ's release 2 years back when Detective Stacy dutifully informed me that he'd gotten out of prison early for good behavior. I had often wondered how he was doing, after hearing the news from Detective Stacy, but figured it best to keep that part of my life in the past, where it belonged.

"I'm good," I said. "How about you? You look good." I didn't know what else to say but the thoughts that ran through my mind. "I mean, you look… healthy." I quickly corrected myself, to clear up any confusion either of them may have had by what I meant to say.

AJ smiled. "Thank you. I've been sober for seven years now. That therapist you sent me really helped me out. I had a lot of pent up shit I didn't want to admit to myself." AJ said to Jasper.

"I'm glad it helped, man." Jasper said, as he pulled me in closer to his side. I could tell in the tone of his voice that he was still on guard.

"I wanted to find you when I got out to say thank you, but I couldn't because of the order of protection you have in place." AJ said, sighing. "I'm really sorry you met me in such a dark time in my life, Carla. You didn't deserve half of the things I put you through." I had many visions of what might happen if I ever ran into AJ again, standing inside a grocery store, hearing him apologize, was never one of them.

"I appreciate the acknowledgment and the apology, AJ." I said, in response.

"My life looks very different now." AJ laughed. "All I do is work, spend time with my fiance and play with the band."

"Fiance?" I asked, curiously.

"Michelle and I are getting married next June. She's a good girl. I think you'd really like her. In fact, she kinda reminds me a bit of you, but in her own way, of course."

"That's wonderful. I'm very happy for you." I said with a smile. I truly was happy for the transformation that seemed to have taken place in AJ's life

"Congrats on your engagement." Jasper said. I felt him release some of the tension in his grip, when he reached out to shake AJ's hand. "That's great news, man."

"Thanks." AJ said in response. "Well, I'd better get going now, she's waiting for me to come home and cook dinner. It was nice to see you."

"It's good to see you, too." I said in response as Jasper and I stood there, watching as he walked away.

Jasper draped his arm around my shoulder. "Well, Angel, it looks like you were right, after all. I guess there's a silver lining for AJ, too!" Jasper said, as we began to make our way over to the cashier to check out.

Chapter 45

Hidden Chapter 17

Lena

W here is he? Why won't he take my calls? I wondered as the phone rang through the line for the 5th time. Still, no answer. *I don't understand it... How can he just abandon me and this baby?* Well, technically, it's not *really* his, but he doesn't know that!

That stupid old geezer security guard really has it coming for not letting me upstairs! I slipped my phone inside the pocket of my jeans and walked across the street. I'm so mad, I could spit bullets!

My heart is beating a mile a minute as I race my way toward the bookstore, where that bitch, Carla works. I was trying to keep her out of this. The fewer people involved, the better, but I don't have much of a choice right now. I stopped to sit down on the bench, outside the bookstore to catch my breath. Maybe I can just follow her. This way, she won't have to see me.

My phone began to buzz inside my pocket. I pulled it out, hoping it was Jasper calling me back. He hasn't returned my calls in over a week. *He has to at some point, right? Especially if I'm supposedly carrying his God damn child! FUCK! It's Sam!*

"Hey baby, how did it go?" Sam asked, sounding hopeful.

"Not good. He changed his pin code and the stupid guard won't let me up! I don't get it! How can he just ignore me, like this? " I replied on the brink of tears. *These damn hormones!* I never cry! Crying is for weak minded people. I learned to suck it up a long time ago, when life got real.

I was 10 years old when I came to the states with my older brother, Dimitri who was 14 and my little sister, Alex who had just turned 6. They told us we were getting a new family to take care of us. *They lied.* We hadn't seen or heard anything from our birth parents ever since! By now, I was sure they were killed off, the day we left for America.

Pfft, it was supposed to be a beautiful place, or so we were told. Our lives had become a living nightmare the moment we stepped foot on American soil. At least for Alex and me. The two of us were sold off as sex slaves while Dimitri got the royal treatment in learning the ropes of the business. But that's all in the past, I'm taking my power back and this money is gonna help me get Alex back! It's too late for Dimitri, he's one of *them* now.

"Don't worry, Baby, we'll figure it out." Sam tried to console me. "I know Jasper. He would never let you abort his baby. He's gonna give you the check, I'll bet my life on it!"

"I hope so. I'll die if anything ever happens to you." I said, lying straight through my teeth. It was a skill I'd picked up in my years of surviving the ugliest form of life, New York had to offer. You'd be surprised at who showed up to have their hands at us. We were just kids. Just thinking about it made me sick to my stomach. When we were old enough, we graduated from pedophiles to men who desired someone older. With that came our freedom to roam the streets a bit, in search of Johns to bring in.

Sam was one of those Johns. I found him at a high stakes poker table in the underground casino, run by the mob we were controlled by. When I found out I was pregnant, Sam offered my escape to Boston with his agenda to get himself out of the jam he was in. I wanted to trust him, but I had learned early on that putting my trust in anyone other than Cami was dangerous. Cami and I roamed the streets together and always had each other's backs. She'd become a second sister to me.

My plan was to get away from New York and get this money so I could come back for Cami and figure out a way to find Alex. We had always dreamed of running away to California, but the scumbags that had us working for them kept all of our money. Every single penny! It was their way of keeping us in line, making sure we came back to a warm bed and food. We had to stay, it was our only chance at survival.

Getting pregnant was something I hadn't planned on, but it served as the perfect scenario for Sam's plan. I knew I was going to have this abortion, regardless, but I needed to get my hands on that check first!

"The same car was parked outside the club again this morning. It has to be them, I just know it!" Sam said. "I was going over the numbers again, and it's just not adding up fast enough. I have to split all the profits with Jasper. We're doing well at the club, but it's just not gonna cut it. These assholes won't give me any more time."

"Did you get a look at who it was?" I asked, wondering if it might be Dimitri.

"No, I turned off all the lights the second I saw them pull up to the curb. I didn't want them to know I was there."

"Alright, well, I guess I'll head that way now. I was going to try and follow Carla to see if she might lead me to Jasper, but I don't think she's here." I said, as I peered through the window of the coffee shop.

"Okay, I'll see you when you get here. Be careful. Come around to the back entrance and whatever you do, don't let them see you."

"I won't. I'm on my way." I said before ending the call with Sam. I took the stairs down to the subway to go meet him at the club.

About the Author

Originally born in Queens, NY, Elisa Ann Pratt currently resides in south Florida with her husband, two teenage sons and three fur babies. She works full time, dealing cards for a living, while pursuing her passion for writing in her spare time.

Her talent was first noticed by friends and family when she began writing poetry as a little girl. In middle school, one of her poems won a contest, landing a spot in the school newspaper.

In high school, she took several creative writing courses and wrote poetry and short stories for fun, mostly entertaining her friends, but also utilizing her writing as an outlet for her most inner thoughts.

Always a hard worker, Elisa took pride in the various hats she wore as a young adult, where she sometimes worked three jobs to make ends meet.

On social media, you'll find she loves to cook, listen to music, take photos and read books. She truly believes we are all gifted with our own unique talent to share with the world and goes out of her way to support anyone with courage to chase their own dreams and aspirations.

Elisa finally feels ready to showcase her writing to a greater audience where she hopes to entertain, inspire and connect with others.

Follow her for updates at: Linktr.ee/elisaannpratt

Also by Elisa Ann Pratt

It is my hope that the underlying message behind The Silver Linings Trilogy has found its way to you.

Even the darkest of souls we encounter are facing demons we know nothing about. If we can find it in our hearts to remember this as we navigate our way through life and offer love and compassion to those people we meet on our journey. Perhaps they too, can find their way out of the darkness and back into the light.

Imagine how valuable a single match is to a candle in a black out. We all hold the power within us to light up the world in love. Every time you look in the mirror, remember just how powerful that light within you truly is and how much it amplifies when you share it with others.

Being a published author is my dream come true. I want to express my deepest gratitude to my readers for being the greatest part of my writing journey. Without you all, none of this is possible.

I have met some amazing people in my Indie Author journey who have found such a special place in my heart. Your support, guidance and love has made this process a deeply enriching experience. I truly love you all from the bottom of my heart.

If you or someone you know is struggling with domestic abuse, please know there are resources available that can help you.

National Domestic Abuse Hot Line
   Available 24/7
   English and Spanish and 200+ other languages with interpretation services
   phone: 800-799-7233
   SMS: Text START to 88788